Magnetic North

The publisher gratefully acknowledges the assistance of
The Ontario Arts Council and the Canada Council for the
Arts.

Canadian Cataloguing in Publications Data
E.R. Sluga
Magnetic North
A Jenny Anttila Book
ISBN: 1-896356-31-1
I. Title

Published by Gutter Press, P.O. Box 600 Station Q
Toronto, Ontario, Canada M4T 2N4
voice (416) 822-8708, fax (416) 822-8709
e-mail: gutter@gutterpress.com

Represented and Distributed in Canada by:
Publishers Group West Canada
250A Carlton Street
Toronto, Ontario, Canada M5L 2L1
Toll Free: 1-800-747-8147, fax (416) 934-1410

Cover Design: 4dt (4 designerly types)
Cover photo: C. Barron
Printed in Canada

Acknowledgements

An excerpt of this book has appeared in Blood &
Aphorisms.

Thanks to my editor Jenny Anttila for her direction and
vision. Also, thanks to Cecil Jensen and Maggie McKee
for their hard work and insight and to Frank Flynn for
his long talks and help in the early stages.

Magnetic North

E.R. Sluga

For Claire and Jack

Magnetic North

Prologue

"Who's that?" My young guard asked, filled with fear. His voice, thin and wispy, caused my heart to stir. If it was someone who was not of the cause, how could he stop them from coming and killing us all? They were all just boys.

The boy who had come into the compound was Wiju, my escort. He identified himself with the right phrase.

"He is on the last patio, near the steps to the river," said my guard. I heard the scraping of metal on a stone floor.

Wiju walked slowly toward the back of the compound. As he moved forward, eyes wide and alert, I could feel him listening for sounds of someone rushing. I had told him, "Just because they seem friendly, does not mean that they are. Remember that some men will sell themselves, their family and all that they believe in for a price. For most men that price is not very high." I remembered the puzzled look on his face as we sat on the high dike between two flooded rice fields. Long, thin, deep canals flowed around us and the other men had put down their rifles and bathed as the afternoon sun hung like a ripe orange, ready to pluck. I explained, "they will sell themselves, but the true price is that they have given themselves to someone else. When they realize that they are lost they have no care and will destroy anything."

He reached the far patio where I lay, curled in a ball like a sleeping child. Around the patio were the fragrant flowers that he must have known since he was a boy. Their pink and white blooms remained year round; his mother and sisters would use them in their daily offerings to the gods. Behind the flowers, on the far side of the patio, was a friend of Wiju's, standing in the shadows. The other boy kept watch as I slept. He held an old rifle left by the Japanese when they had fought for this same land only two years before.

I heard Wiju slide his sandals from his feet and walk onto the patio. His small feet squeaked as he neared me.

"Mister, wake up," he said in his newly learned English. "Time go." He mimicked the words I had trained him to say. I slowly raised myself onto an elbow and stretched. I had slept little and felt weary. I turned to face Wiju.

"Thank you." I raised myself first to a sitting position and then stood. I looked out onto the rice paddies. A hint of the morning sun glowed purple in the distance by the sacred mountain. I allowed myself the opportunity to relax and await the sun. Soon it would rise slowly along the northern slope until it was full and orange. Soon a new day would begin. A better day, one that was filled with promise and not fear. One that would mean a better life for my young friends.

"We go, sun come," said Wiju, pulling me from my meditation. I looked down at the river that flowed quietly in the lush green valley below where we stood. I walked toward Wiju and sat on the step of the patio.

"Sit," I said lightly tapping the space beside me. "First we'll see the sun and then we'll go." Wiju became nervous. We both knew I had to be gone by sunup, down by the river, moving west, to the meeting place. Wiju looked at his friend holding the rifle. The teenager shrugged. Reluctantly, Wiju sat beside me and looked out onto the fields of rice paddies and past to the sacred mountain where the sun began to rise along the northern slope.

Down along the river we moved slowly, walking with purpose. Wiju led and I followed. Mothers and their children bathed. The children ran naked through the shallows while the mothers, young with smiles that were broad and white, giggled as we passed. My eyes stayed fixed on the back of the boy that led me to the meeting place. Twice we heard the noise of jeeps on the roads high above and threw ourselves into the thick brush under the huge trees. Each time it was a false alarm. We remained unseen. As we walked along, I looked into the small caves and sheltered places that seemed to be in every small ravine and river valley. Only months before, these spaces were filled with foreign soldiers fighting a bloody battle against each other as the local people looked on, hoping to avoid the death around them. Now it was the people themselves who used the hiding places, hoping to avoid the men in jeeps who travelled along the roads.

After walking for almost two hours, the valley opened to a larger river in a larger valley. There, next to a tall tree with long arms that reached down from its top to touch the earth, the men we had come to meet sat eating cold rice.

"You have come," said the leader, his back to the tree, his men around him. "We were not certain." One of the leader's men said something harsh to Wiju. The boy stepped back in fear.

"I was slow to move," I said to the leader. "It will not happen again."

The leader looked at his man with dark moist eyes that made the anger in his face disappear, then motioned to us to sit.

"Eat," he said showing a large bowl with rice. I took some rice in a large leaf from a neatly cut pile – like paper plates – and gave it to Wiju, then I took another leaf for myself. I stood and walked over to the river and sat down, away from the open so that I could see the water flow in front of me. Further down children played. A small boat with an old man drifted by. The man was fishing. The leader came over and sat with me.

"We go to the mountain today," said the leader – the place that had been talked about as the spot for the meeting of all the small bands. We would be coming together to create the army that the leader and the other older men had been talking about.

"Tell me again," I said to him as he finished his rice, "why is the mountain sacred?"

The leader smiled. His face was older than his years. The scars of the war seemed to be everywhere on his brown skin. But his eyes held no fear or remorse. They glowed and made his face beautiful.

"You have been here many months now," he said and looked away. I nodded; it had already been a year since I had arrived and found the leader. "The mountain to our people is holy, it is next to the gods," he said. He put his hand on my knee. "All the land is holy, the mountain, the trees, the river. It is all part of the gods. But the mountain is closest to the gods."

I watched the river, the muddy water flowing.

"It is not this way where I come from," I said to the leader.

His eyes turned sad and he looked at me. I knew he still did not understand me and why I was here, why I was fighting the demons inside me here, alongside his people. He smiled again.

"That is too bad." He turned to watch the river with me.

"Here, you understand what it is to live," I said after searching my heart for something to say. I bowed my head and rubbed at the stubble that was my hair. I looked up at him. He slowly waved a fly away from his face and smiled at me. Again I could see that he felt sad for me, and I realized that I was not a man in all things. He knew that perhaps my heart and my courage were that of a man, but I longed to be connected with something that would fill my soul and make it grow and feel complete.

He had read, while he and his comrades were in exile, of our lost spirit, our dead God. He had seen it in the busy streets, filled with machines that seemed to be more important than the people they served. To the leader, I was a boy really, trying to become whole. I was like the world I had come from, passionate, strong and fearless but unaware that the journey of life needed commitment, not to a cause but a commitment to life. How many men lived their lives without being complete? How could they be so removed, the soul without connection to the God of their land?

Finally, after looking at me for a long time, he responded to what I had said, choosing his words carefully, "You are no different than we." He sighed and bowed his head. "We all wish our lives to be better, for our world to be better, Say Sil," he said, drawing my name out into two complete words, each with their own life, his pronunciation of Cecil turned into a child-like rhyme. "What we fight for here is to make our lives – my life, my child's life – better. We can be wrong. Maybe we do this and we make our world worse. This is man's weakness. We wish life to be easy as this river flowing in front of us. Many men think – especially men like you, I've lived among such men – that to achieve this they must build a river for themselves and then control the river, make it do as they wish. They need to be strong, to let the river flow as it will."

There was a silence between us. He took up a stick beside him and drew in the mud with it, humming a prayer. I leaned forward and put my hand in the cool brown water that rushed in front of us. The power of its current passed through my fingers. I raised myself up and put both hands into the water, cupped them and splashed my face and head. I felt the sleep in my eyes wash away. The water rolled down my head and shirt. I was awake now as the river flowed by me, over me and then – in me.

Magnetic North

Chapter 1

The morning sky was filled with warm air that hovered over the dark green water. It wasn't daybreak yet, but Frank could already feel the heat from the sun that sat hidden behind the tree line. Yesterday was the hottest day he had ever experienced, beyond anything he had found in Cairo or Bangkok. But, the heat yesterday was different. There was no haze or smog. This was clean, pure sky, and the sun shone through it without the filter of smoke, exhaust fumes and the breath of millions of people struggling under the oppressive heat.

The tin coffee cup had cooled enough for him to grasp the tiny handle and bring it carefully to his lips. He blew on the liquid and took a sip. He sat and waited for the sun to rise, alone on the dock of Willie's friend's cabin, beside a lake with a Native name that he could not remember.

Willie had made much of the beauty of the northern sunrise. How the sky illuminated the trees and water, and how they helped, in turn, to make the sky seem more blue than could be possible. Willie was always rational, grounded. When she usually spoke, her eyes were clear, purposeful. But, when she spoke of her days spent north of the city, she looked at Frank in a way that he imagined all poets must look: distant and detached from themselves and the world around them. Speaking of something greater than any single moment, greater than anything mortal, something eternal. It was Willie's dreamy remembrance, her eyes filled with the glow of the many previous sunrises, that had him awake and out so early.

Morning was not his part of the day. That had always belonged to other people. His parents seemed alive and fresh in the mornings when they woke him for school. His mother had always said he was a good baby and he would sleep all morning. In high school, the athletes were always there early, pushing or running or lifting. Not Frank, who was often laughed at as he entered the classroom, late again, his name called for the daily trip to the vice-principal's office. At university he would see the science and engineering students already on their way home after a full day of classes. At two PM, he would be on his way to his first lecture of the day, making sure to arrange his timetable in that manner. So much of the day gone. Even working at the paper enabled him to sleep late. When he first started, he happily took the night sports duty, waiting by the phone for calls from officials of local amateur sports teams. "North York 3, Mississauga 2 in double overtime," they would say. Frank often wanted to chat with the mainly older gentlemen who, almost to a man, dropped their 'G's'. "Four – nothin" rather than "nothing". "Everythin' was goin' by'em." But they, tired from a long night of "cheerin' on the local boys," would decline.

But he was up now, searching for that first light. He couldn't sleep and hadn't since the day he had said yes to his new position. What did he know about being a columnist, having opinions? To be so certain. To be able to see things so clearly. He had seen the journalists who wrote those weekly pieces. How enormously satisfied they were, how absolute. He would hide in facts, in the story. The plot that unfolded mattered to him most, not how it landed on the shoulders of those who read the piece. He enjoyed taking on anything that would come, no matter who the villain and who the wronged. Political sides meant nothing. The story was the thing.

He looked at the dark lake and tried to make out his surroundings. The dock reached about 20 feet from the shore. The cabin was built back in the forest, away from the water's edge. To his left, the lake widened to almost half a mile before it ended about two miles from where he sat. To his right, the lake pinched in until it rounded to a bay only a stone's throw away. The opposite shore wasn't far, maybe 100 feet. The lake was rimmed by rocks and tall pines. The trees were large and, to Frank, who knew little about the forest, seemed to be very old. Some had fallen into the water. There was no sandy beach, but he liked the granite outcrops.

This was "cottage country." Frank had heard about it all his life, but it was always a great Canadian mystery to him. His parents weren't cottagers. They hadn't grown up in Canada, and the idea of a summer getaway was as foreign to them as many other customs here. Camps and canoe trips weren't part of his early years. They had not bothered getting involved. Tied to the urban immigrant community, on Saturday mornings his father was more likely to walk down Arlington Avenue, along St. Clair, to his favourite café. There, he would find a comfortable chair, drink small cups of thick, strong coffee, and read the newspaper.

Frank's father was a reluctant follower of politics. It had been that way since his escape from his native Yugoslavia – or what was Yugoslavia – through the days in the many camps awaiting his turn for the proper papers and passage to a place where he could make some money, hoping to use it to move on to America. Devastated and confused when he was rejected, he was elated and even more confused when, upon arriving in Canada, he became happier than he could ever imagine. Now he read his paper every day, from start to finish. He cherished the information it brought as much as those for which the information seemed trivial and who took it for granted. He could hardly believe his luck when Frank came home and told him that he had a job as a reporter for a national newspaper.

Magnetic North

Finally, he could access information from the source, before it was common knowledge. Frank never had the heart to explain that this was not the case.

Frank's father would stay most of the morning and early afternoon, reading his paper and talking with neighbours, usually in their own language, speaking about what Frank had written. Frank's father could speak Russian, Italian, German, Croatian, French and some Flemish, and often joked that he had forgotten which one was his own native tongue. But to each of the café patrons he would show Frank's byline and explain that this was his son.

Frank found himself looking deeply into his cup. He took a short sip. He could feel the footsteps of someone on the dock. He knew it was Willie but pretended not to notice. She touched his back. He acted surprised.

"What are you doing up so early?" he asked.

"I heard you get up and thought I'd join you." Willie said.

"Want a sip?" He showed her the cup. She reached down and took it. "Careful. It's hot." he said. The sleeves of her sweater were over her hands so that only the tips of her slender fingers were showing. She whistled her breath across the warm liquid.

"Come to see the sunrise?" she asked him. She knew the restlessness of his sleep and the turmoil he was going through. She had tried to tell him that it would be alright. They would talk and she tried to let him know that he would work things out. Nothing seemed to work.

"I've been told it isn't all that bad," he said, smiling back. She took a sip. Apart from the sweater, the only other article of clothing she had on was her bathing suit. Willie liked to take early morning swims. She spoke of them like religion. As though it was an act of worship to plunge into the frigid early morning water, purifying and cleansing herself. The quick and full cold on her body was a form of suffering and pleasure. Sacrifice and acceptance. He had never seen it, never watched

16

as she worshiped. He had wanted to. Each time she would speak of her days under the great northern sky, in the early morning, standing over misty water, he would long to be with her there. But he had always worked Saturdays. He was never free when she went away with friends, to her father's place in Muskoka, or to her mother's on Georgian Bay. He had wanted to come with her, to see the sun rise, and watch her swim. He had wanted it as he had rarely wanted anything before.

"Here's the sun," she said, nudging him with her knee. Frank turned and looked at her long, well-muscled legs. He followed the line of her calf to the back of her thigh, up to her buttocks, which showed beneath the sweater she wore.

On the other end of the lake, there was a glow above the trees. The lake was small and had no horizon of water. The rounded top of the large burning ball peeked through a small V-shaped opening at the top of the treeline. Willie moved to the end of the dock, sat down, and thrust her legs out over the water, waiting for the sun to reach them from across the lake. It happened suddenly. The pure orange light bathed them in a pool of fire. The warmth struck their faces. The light made Frank squint.

"The sun hit me first," said Willie, in a voice that made Frank sorry not to have known her as a little girl. It was a sweet tone, held together with a small giggle.

"Time to go in," she said, getting up from where she was sitting. "Are you coming?" There was a grin on her face.

"You have got to be kidding," he said. She let out a laugh.

"Come on," said Willie, "this is a real Canadian thing to do. It's the greatest feeling."

For a moment, Frank considered it. A conversion? He would throw off his clothes, leap in, and join in her ceremony. Her pagan religion based on the worship of water and cold. He smiled at her again. Although the thought was appealing, he was reluctant.

"I know feelings that are a whole lot better," he said smiling at her. "You play camper today. I'll be the counsellor."

Willie shook her head.

"Getting up this early was effort enough," he continued.

She looked at him as the born-again do towards those who have not felt the presence of their Saviour. It made Frank feel lonely, as though he were missing and could not be found.

Willie took off the sweater. Her bathing suit hung from her like a plastic bag, so worn it was see-through.

"Well, well," said Frank, tugging at the material, "is this a hand-me-down or something?"

"No," she said proudly. "This is a relic of the Willie of summers past."

"Why not get rid of this thing, get yourself one of those two-piece jobs that your friend was wearing yesterday, what's her name?" asked Frank.

"You mean Sue?" Willie rolled her eyes. "Not me, my friend. I've got myself a man, and besides, I can't give this up, I wore it when I was a teenager at camp." She giggled again. Frank laughed as well.

She stood at the edge of the dock. Frank moved back slightly to avoid the possible splash. The sun was completely over the trees now. The early morning heat signalled another day of sweating and looking for shade. Willie's arms swung back and forth by her side. She was getting herself into a rhythm. It was as though if she swung her arms long and hard enough, the force would pull her into the water without her being able to stop. Swing, swing, swing. The thing was set in motion. It was a matter of time. Swing, swing, swing... She was in. She was under the water for a moment and then she surfaced.

"Yooouuuah!" she screamed out. Praise the Lord, thought Frank.

"Cold?" he asked smugly.

"Glorious." She turned, head down in the water, and began to swim. Frank heard a noise on the other end of the lake. He craned his neck toward the sound. He could hear a human voice muttering.

"Sounds like someone's over there," he said loudly, half to Willie who couldn't hear him, and half to himself.

There was a small splash. On the far side of the lake, which was only about one hundred feet, the silhouette of a man stood knee deep in the water, trying to pick something out of it without going in any further. He moved slowly. Willie continued to swim into the lake. Frank looked at her to see if she had noticed the man, but she was busy communing. The man retrieved what he was after and walked out of the water.

"Hey!" Frank called out to him. The figure stopped and turned. He looked at Frank for a moment, staring, then turned and went back into the woods.

* * *

When he returned to the cabin, Frank was surprised to see that most of the others were awake, showing the effects of their varied behaviours from the night before. At a table in the corner, two girls – one was Sue, the other's name had escaped Frank – spoke excitedly about taking two weeks at the end of the summer to canoe up to the camp they had gone to as kids. They were beautiful, with a youthful look to them. They smiled brightly and their eyes lit up when they talked about their days as campers.

Sam, one of the drunkards from the night before, lay asleep on the small couch in front of the fireplace, crumpled in an unhealthy manner that appeared to Frank as if he had been shot dead and then fell into that position. He was tall and wide, with a large belly from many nights of drinking too much. Jonathan, the cabin's owner, stood erect by the stove. No one seemed to notice Frank as he walked into the kitchen.

"Any coffee?" asked Frank as he approached Jonathan.

"Yup." Without turning, Jonathan pointed to where a pot gurgled. The cabin was given to him by an old aunt who had died without an heir. Her husband had fought in the Boer War and upon returning was given, as were all the Canadian volunteers of that war, his choice of two hundred acres of crown land. Her husband, being wealthy and without the need of a home or a field, decided to choose this parcel so that he could go moose hunting. Now it was Jonathan's, although he hardly used the place. It was a long way from the city and underdeveloped as far as cottage country went. The province never gave up the land around it. There wasn't another cottage for miles. Jonathan preferred the more social cottage districts of Muskoka or Georgian Bay. There, near Port Carling or Pointe au Baril, you could boat to the neighbours' for drinks before dinner, go to a dance at the club, or golf. This lake was wild and isolated. But, once a year Jonathan came up to see if the place was "still standing" as he put it and would invite anyone that wanted to come along.

"Jonathan, I saw some guy on the other end of the lake," said Frank as he poured a cup of coffee. "I thought you didn't have any neighbours?"

"We don't," said Jonathan. Frank looked at him. He was tall and well-built with a square jaw. He was well-liked and successful beyond any dream that Frank had ever had. Frank couldn't help but smile when he looked at him. There was a natural look to him that was both idyllic and rugged. It was as if he had stepped out of a military recruiting poster or one of the communist party posters that the Marxist Leninist Society at the university had on the crowded office walls. Strong and virtuous, lean and handsome, pure and beyond reproach. The hero for the ages.

"There are fisherman here from time to time, but not many," he said, stirring up some bacon in the pan. "This place doesn't get many visitors, but some of the locals come in to fish in the summer or hunt in the winter."

"Well this is a long way from..." Frank didn't finish his sentence. He wasn't quite sure where they were except that they had driven a long way, taking roads that were progressively worse until they finally drove up what seemed like a dried river bed to where they parked.

"Yeah," said Jonathan, "we're in the middle of nowhere. I'm not quite sure why I even come. I mean, each year they call the local volunteer search and rescue out to find someone who didn't make it back. It gives the local boys a chance to skip off work and play commando with their ATVs. They never find them though but they look for weeks. Last year it was a group of three adventure types that wanted to walk an old trail from a map they had dug up in an archive. It was some early trapping route. They never saw them again."

Jonathan fumbled again with his cooking.

"Shit," Frank tried to imagine why someone would want to risk their lives simply to follow a trail through the forest.

"What sort of fish would he be after?" asked Frank thinking it was a good question and pleased he had come up with it.

Jonathan was only half paying attention. He was trying to pour the bacon grease into a small can. "Frank, I thought you weren't an outdoors man. The fishing on this lake is for trout. He'd be trolling for lake trout – Shit!" said Jon. Grease poured onto the counter. "Anyway, shit, damn grease, all this land is open to the public, anyone can use it whenever they want. Well, you can't hunt at the wrong time of the year or anything like that." Jonathan reached for two eggs, broke them, and poured the white and yellow into the hot pan.

"But he wasn't in a boat or canoe or anything, he was just on the bank," said Frank.

Jonathan looked up at Frank for a moment, "Just on the bank?" he said, puzzled. It was as though the statement made no sense. Why would someone just be standing by the lake's shore?

"Sounds like that ghost you told me about," said a voice from the corner.

It was Brian, hiding behind dark sunglasses. He was a

friend of Jonathan's. Frank didn't like him much. Granted, he hadn't really given him much of an opportunity, but he liked to think he could figure people out quickly. It was just after sunrise and the guy already had a beer in his hand. "What do you think, Stacks?" he asked slowly. Frank felt like throwing his coffee cup at him.

"Yeah, right," said Jonathan with a laugh.

"What?" asked Frank, confused and uncomfortable with the passing of coded messages.

"Could be, Stacks. You might be haunted. Mr. Frank might have just seen a ghost." Frank could feel his blood pressure rising.

"Gimme a break," said Jonathan, scooping the eggs out of the pan and onto his plate.

"What ghost?" asked Frank quietly, hoping only Jonathan would hear. It made Frank feel like a child, but he wanted nothing to do with the lump of shit in the chair. It didn't work. Brian heard him and walked over to them.

"Always the newshound, eh?" he said, reeking of gin from the night before. Martini after martini had gone down his throat the entire evening. As he finished the full bottle, he talked about how the country was falling apart. How there was no one to lead, that the ills of society could be blamed on divorce, immigration and the lack of commitment to facing the global economy. His performance forced the girls to bed early. Sam drank to escape him. Jonathan smiled, nodded, and was a good host. Frank spent the night sipping a beer and whispering remarks to Willie. Each time she laughed they would be shot angry looks.

"I suppose so," said Frank. The meekness of his response made him angry. He wanted nothing more than to show how opposed he was to the drunk, opposed to everything he said, and everything that he did. But, for some reason he couldn't.

"Tell him the story, Stacks. Maybe Mr. Frank should grab his notebook and pen." Frank looked at the counter. The grease began to congeal.

"Well, there's an old story about some guy. He was up here hunting or something and his plane went down. They never found him, the pilot, or the plane. It was years ago. He was a bigwig in the city. Anyway, my parents used to joke that his ghost haunted the area. But that was just to give us a good scare before bed."

"We used it on the girls we'd bring up here too," said Brian.

"We're nervous enough just being up here alone with you guys," said Sue from the table in the corner. They giggled. None of the men remarked back.

"Anyway, there's more to the story, but I can't remember it now," said Jonathan, putting ketchup on his eggs. Willie came in. Her sweater was wrapped loosely around her waist like a towel. Her bathing suit lay like wet paper against her body. The material, see-through from years of use, left little to imagine. Brian stared at her through his sunglasses.

"Hey Willie," he said, with a sinister smile on his face. He walked toward her sauntering.

"Cover up would ya Willie, no one needs to see that," said Jonathan, cutting Brian off with his words.

Willie looked down at herself. She took the sweater from her waist and pulled it over her head and around her body.

"You boys can't take the sight of a pair of nipples," she said once the sweater was in place.

"Now, now," said Jonathan. "None of your feminist ways around here. We are strictly non-political, isn't that right, Frank?" Jonathan asked, nudging Frank.

"You bet," said Frank. He felt like an idiot. Why couldn't he come up with something clever to say?

Brian continued, undeterred.

"Willie, we were just talking about your pain-in-the-ass cousin, Hayes." Willie looked confused for a moment. She wasn't quite sure what he was talking about. Frank was also confused.

"Which Hayes?" asked Willie. She walked toward Frank. "About two hundred people in my family have the last name Hayes."

"You know, Hayes. The cousin who went missing," he said. Frank was astonished at the drunk's knowledge of Willie's family.

"Oh yeah, that's his name," said Jonathan, reminded.

There was a look of understanding in Willie's face. "Brian isn't boring you with old stories, is he? It seems that no matter how much you drink, you don't get any more interesting," she said. Again, there was laughter from the corner. Willie turned and made a face at them and they began to laugh harder, their entire bodies moving. Willie pushed past Frank toward the kitchen. She poured herself a cup of coffee. "Hayes died in a hunting accident in the early sixties," she said. She found the sugar tin and sprinkled some into the cup without a spoon. She took a knife from the counter and stirred the coffee.

* * *

Driving Willie's car down to the city later that morning, Willie beside him reading some papers that she had meant to go over during the weekend, Frank couldn't help but take in the beauty of the Canadian Shield. As a child Frank would spend hours in the park, the only green space he really knew. Even through university he never really left Toronto. No school trips to the wilderness, no camping adventures with his friends. Now, looking closely at the pines and granite and water around him, he couldn't help feeling he had missed out. The trees and the roads and the sky seemed untamed. There was an awe-inspiring clearness.

Huge power towers stood along the road like children in line at school, each one connected by a long wire to keep them together. Frank realized that even in a place so remote those long thin wires could connect the people of this area with the rest of the world. The world then seemed very small. He thought of those names that he had learned in history class, MacKenzie and Thompson and the rest of them, not knowing what lay ahead and not knowing if they would ever return. That was gone now, Frank thought to himself. Now the power lines, buzzing with electricity, were life lines. Each person was plugged into the world.

As they drove the long straight road, electrical poles stood at attention, at the service of the people who lived in the houses along the road. Each line connecting each house with every other house in the country and in the world. It was all remarkable. Frank noticed that all the lines went south from the road. No lines went north. It must be all crown land up there, he thought to himself.

Willie had a knack of making suggestions to Frank that made them seem more than just interesting. At times, she'd even have him excited. Whether it was that she always seemed to talk about dinner get - togethers when he was reading the sports section or would talk about a new play just after they had finished making love, her bright smile and the way ideas made her body dance in small slow figure eights had Frank agreeing to almost anything. Not until the day was upon him did he realize that a few weeks earlier, while she was massaging his back, he had agreed to dinner at her aunt's.

Now Willie sat in the big leather chair in his living room with her legs crossed; she wore a short black wrap skirt. The white shirt she wore had a frill on the sleeves and she was covered in gold jewelry. He could tell that she had her push-up bra on. She looked casual and sexy. Frank loved that. He sat across from her in his bathrobe. He had decided to take a shower when he got home to wake himself up.

Willie wiggled her shoe on the end of her toe and looked at him from under her bangs.

"Are you getting ready soon?" she asked. He looked at her toe. His first thought had nothing to do with getting dressed;

just the opposite. He watched the shoe bounce from side to side without saying anything. His head bobbed with the rhythm.

"Forget it," she said in a semi-stern voice. Frank frowned in a mock childlike way. "Go get dressed!" She kicked her shoe at him. Frank caught the shoe and tossed it back. He looked at the clock on the VCR. It was getting late. As much as having dinner with Willie's aunt was a chore for him, he didn't mind that much if he was in a good mood. He was feeling up to it tonight. He went upstairs to get dressed.

Dinner at Willie's aunt's could be anything from a pleasant pain to downright torture. Frank wasn't good with the rituals of eating. He had grown up in a family that was kinetic in its relations with one another. They didn't eat together much. When they did, it was fast. Discussions weren't necessary. He remembered times in his younger years, before he had reached his teens, when his mother would eat standing up as she busily served dinner to the rest of his family. When they arrived at the table the food was ready. People began regardless of who was there. His father would always be last. He would sit down and Frank's mother would serve him. There would be little communication. There was no ritual of carving meat or serving food. There was little if any dessert. Someone would do the dishes as the rest dispersed.

It was different in Willie's family and very different for Willie's aunt. She enjoyed the ceremony and wished it regularly. Frank always sensed that she had little to say to him except for during dinner, when she was alight with conversation. She always dressed for dinner, especially on Sunday evening, with her gold jewelry dangling from her thin neck and even thinner wrists. She would put the food on platters and would serve each person herself from her chair at the head of the table. This was her chair. She would serve each person, painfully questioning each portion of the meal. "Now Frank," she would say with a serving spoon in hand, "how much squash would you like?" Frank, almost confused by the question the first time he heard it, replied, "How much do you have?" hoping to make a joke. It was taken politely and was then asked again.

The doorman at her aunt's posh building greeted Willie and called Frank "Pete" as he had done since he first met Frank. Willie had wanted to correct him but Frank didn't want to embarrass the fellow in the blue uniform. Frank wasn't comfortable with the hired help around these places. They were too eager to please and too polite in the old-fashioned way. He often wondered how they descended into the position. Willie had scolded Frank the first time he had said this. She felt he was being hard on the men who manned the doors and the desk at the building. They were working for a living like he was and he shouldn't judge them. Frank told her that it was rather ironic that she came across as such a friend of the working man.

As Willie and Frank took the elevator to the floor her aunt lived on, Frank recalled the first time they had gone to dinner there. He hadn't known what to think. Willie hadn't told him that since her mother had moved to Florida, her aunt, her mother's younger sister, had taken a keen interest in Willie's life. She called almost daily and always wanted her over for dinner. Willie had talked to her mother about it but she couldn't do anything. Her aunt had a strong will.

That first night, Frank had trouble with the very personal questions she had asked. They were questions about his family, his job, and his future plans. With every answer, Willie's aunt seemed to become more somber. She would look at Willie, her eyes darkening. Finally, in what seemed to be an admission of defeat, she said in her husky voice, gruff from years of smoking, "Well," and then after a long pause, "Welcome Frank, welcome."

Willie fixed Frank's tie before they got to the door and smoothed her skirt. Frank knocked on the door with one loud rap.

"Frank," said Willie with a look that meant, *I wish you would stop doing that.* She walked in.

"Aunt Trish," she called out. There was a cloud of smoke in the hallway. Willie grumbled under her breath. Frank let out a mock cough and waved at the air.

"Anyone in here?" he said in a quiet voice, pretending to have trouble seeing through the smoke. Willie didn't laugh.

"Hello," said Willie's aunt from around the corner. Frank and Willie walked into the apartment. Margaret Stanley was sitting on a large wingback chair. With her was a gentleman Frank had never met before. Both of them were smoking cigarettes. The ashtray on the coffee table was filled.

"Hello, Willie darling," said Willie's aunt. Her name was Margaret but she liked to be called Trish, short for Patricia, her middle name. Frank wasn't comfortable calling people of her age by their first names. He just tried to catch her attention before saying anything.

"Hello Frank," she said drawing out the "a" in Frank until it seemed almost a full minute before she reached the "k".

"Hello," said Frank.

"Willie, you remember Richard Rankin," said Trish with a wry smile. Her smile was one of a university girl introducing her boyfriend to the other girls at the sorority. Frank thought that they must be sleeping together. The way she said it was too coy.

Richard was in his mid-sixties. He had a full head of grey hair and it was slicked back with what must have been a full jar of gel. He was casually dressed, but his clothes were fashionable and immaculate. From the cut of his blazer, to the ascot, right down to the classic line of his shoes, the man's attire was incredible. What he was wearing probably cost as much as Frank's entire wardrobe. Frank had always wanted to dress in that elegant Noel Cowardesque way: ascots and satin dinner jackets.

Willie looked as if she hadn't a clue who he was.

"Of course, how are you Mr. Rankin," she said, reaching out her hand to shake his. He took it, pulled her close, and gave her a kiss on the lips. It startled her.

"How are you, Willie?" he asked in a vague English accent.

"Fine," she said. She moved away from him and turned to Frank.

"This is Frank Medved," said Willie, rolling her eyes.

"How'd you do, Frank?"

"Hello," said Frank, shaking Richard's hand.

"Well, dinner is almost ready," said Trish. Frank had already learned that this was code for "You are late."

"Sorry. We're a little late," Willie said. Frank looked at his watch and realized that they were actually early. Time in its logical, linear sense mattered little to Trish. Frank thought it was because she had so little to do with all of hers.

"Well, we should sit and eat," said Trish. She butted out her cigarette gracefully with little movement, walked over to the table and leaned on one of the side chairs. "Frank, you sit here. Willie, you sit there. Richard, you're here." She smiled at Richard and he smiled back.

"Wherever you want me," said Richard in a low voice that let out a wisp of smoke from his lungs. Frank was now sure that they were sleeping together and the thought intrigued him. He wondered what sex was like over the age of sixty. He imagined the two of them naked. All that skin hanging down. He tried to picture them in bed, arms around one another.

"Frank, what is it you do?" asked Richard. He had asked Toronto's second favourite question after "What is your name?" Richard's accent puzzled Frank. It wasn't English but it had the drawn tones of one.

"I'm a newspaper reporter," said Frank, placing his napkin across his lap.

"He's a columnist," said Willie.

"Yes, columnist." It was still hard for Frank to say. He wasn't sure he or the newspaper wanted the situation to continue.

"Oh." said Richard. "Are you with *The Globe*?"

Frank smiled. "No," he said, flatly tired of having answered the same question from many of Willie's friends and family.

Richard frowned. "Well, I suppose it doesn't matter which paper you work for." He tried to hide what he really thought. "They're all good." He turned to look at Willie.

"Willie, what are you doing now?" he asked. Neither responded to the snub Frank had just received.

"I'm a Senior Associate with MacLaughlan, Castlefield and Grant." Impressed, Richard raised his eyebrows.

"I must say you have done well for yourself," said Richard as Trish came from the kitchen with a platter of food and placed it on the table. She brought out another platter and then brought out plates that had been warming in the oven. Frank chuckled to himself. He shook his head and Willie caught him. He winked at her and she winked back.

"Now, Frank," said Trish, sitting down again. She seemed to hang onto the "a" longer than usual. "Richard is an old friend of mine. We knew each other long before he moved to London, long before and we've kept in touch." Frank took this to mean they had had an ongoing affair for some time. Trish had not meant it that way, he was sure, but he felt it added colour to her drab life.

"Really," he said, not knowing exactly how to respond.

"Oh, yes," said Richard. "Trishie and I go a long way back. Back before she was married, in fact."

"That's right," said Trish. Frank saw Willie look at her aunt but she did not comment. She didn't like getting involved with the ongoing family politics. Frank looked at Richard and then at Trish. They were stealing little glances. Once Trish stuck out her tongue at him in a playful way. He wondered if women her age still gave blow jobs. That would be something to see. Frank imagined Trish on her knees in front of Richard on that huge king - size bed in her apartment. Her head bobbing up and down on Richard's penis. Willie was wonderful at giving blow jobs. Frank wondered if that was a genetic or a learned thing. Some girls that had given Frank blow jobs had liked it. They had actually asked him if they could give him a blow job.

Psychologists might have a problem with that, thought Frank. He was sure that some would find problems with women who liked giving blow jobs. Perhaps they were abused children or had fathers they couldn't please or something like that. Then there were the women who swallowed. They must be really screwed up. Frank looked at Trish arranging the platters on the table. He was sure that, if she did give blow jobs, she swallowed. Trish was a woman who didn't do things in half measures.

Trish began serving and they all waited politely as she did. Once they all had their plates in front of them they began to eat. The conversation was mostly about Richard and what he was doing. Frank learned that he had made a lot of money selling North American electrical technology to the underdeveloped world during the boom period right after the war. He had spent a lot of time in the Middle East, especially in Egypt. Egypt was wonderful then, he said. The country was beautiful and the people so polite and willing. It was a shame that Nazar had been such a problem. But he was a great man. Richard had actually met him on a couple of occasions.

"Were you in the war?" asked Frank casually.

"No," said Richard, "I was just a little too young. It was over just after my eighteenth birthday. I didn't see any fighting but I helped at home."

"Richard was in the cadets at the College," said Trish, "but he never went over."

Frank thought of his own father working for the Partisans at thirteen, carrying the mail for them and then later fighting in the mountains by the Italian border. Being with the cadets at "College" sounded pretty good.

The discussion continued. Richard talked about his travels, which included long and delightful stays in almost all of the third world countries where he exploited their vast electric power potential. He had been through all of South America and a lot of Southeast Asia. He had been in Vietnam just before the war started.

Frank was getting bored and he wanted to get away from the details of Richard's post-war exploitation tour. He looked at Trish until he could catch her eye and the appropriate lull in the conversation occurred.

"I was wondering," he said, looking at her as she held a piece of chicken to her mouth, "I was wondering about your cousin, a man by the name of Hayes."

Trish placed the chicken into her mouth and chewed twice. "Hayes, which Hayes dear? There are many." Frank looked at Willie, not sure which one they had spoken about over the weekend.

"He was the one who died up north on a fishing trip," said Willie, helping to clarify.

"That was Ford Hayes," said Richard, looking at Willie.

"Ford Hayes, what a name," said Frank, taking a sip of wine.

"Cecil Rutherford Hayes," said Trish, leaning forward and clasping her hands together as if she were about to pray. Perhaps it was because she was about to talk about the dead. More likely it was because she was about to talk about her family.

"He was my cousin, although I never really knew him very well. Richard might have known him better." She looked at Richard.

"Well, we were at school together," said Richard. "We weren't great friends or anything. He didn't have much to do with many of the boys there. He was always doing something or other to annoy people. Sort of like your employer, Frank. Have you read Harold Stone's autobiography? Interesting stuff."

"No," said Frank. He hadn't read it. Wasn't it enough that he had to work for him?

"Why are you asking about Ford?" Asked Trish, seeming very familiar with the man now.

"Well, we were up north..." began Frank, until Willie cut in.

"Oh, someone told us about him the other day," she said. Frank didn't know why she had cut him off.

"Up north where?" asked Trish.

"Nowhere, Aunt Trish," said Willie, looking away from her.

"Frank, where were you?" she asked him. Frank knew something was going on and didn't know how to respond. Willie broke in again.

"We were at Jonathan's cottage. We went up on a whim," she said. Frank knew she was lying. They had planned it for a while.

"Oh, I see," said Trish. "So, you went north after all. I thought you couldn't come to my place because you were busy working. But now I see that you had other plans. So, I rush down, dragging poor Richard with me, so that we might have some time together. My dear, this is just too much," she said getting up.

"Aunt Trish, we went on a whim," she said again and looked at Frank for support.

"Yes," Frank said stumbling, "it was a last-minute thing."

Trish went into the kitchen. Willie got up and followed her. She looked at Frank, shutting the door behind them.

Frank and Richard sat for a time looking awkwardly at each other until Frank finally spoke out of sheer panic.

"So, you knew this Hayes fellow," he said, more as a statement than a question, in a way that sounded not very much like himself. He would never use the word "fellow". Frank had a feeling Richard didn't mind talking, so Frank gave him the opportunity.

"Oh yes, Ford and I were old friends," said Richard, getting up and walking to the sideboard to pour himself a drink. Frank wondered how Hayes had gone from being someone at school to an old friend.

"Scotch? Or are you a 'port man?'" he asked with a smile Frank didn't like. There was nothing about Richard that Frank liked.

"Scotch. No ice."

Frank looked at Richard as he poured. He was arrogant and slimy. He was one of those men who talked about things that they had seen or heard, great things that they were only witness to, but acted as though they had played an integral part in them. They were like priests or sports reporters, conveying ideas and events as though they were their own. Confidently dispensing judgment as though it were some right. This was Richard. Here was a man that had gone through life being in a certain place at a certain time and because of it he was wealthy. Men like him were part of a small generation, born into a changing world. Their path made clear by their older rivals dying. Their availability to power accentuated because the women's revolution had not really begun yet.

Richard brought the drinks over into the living room and he and Frank sat down. Frank sat on the couch, sinking in to the point where he thought he might never be able to get up. Richard sat in the old leather wingback and crossed his legs. His toe pointed out and Frank could see the sole of his shoe. It looked as though it had never touched concrete.

"Now, let's see," he said, taking a sip of his drink. Frank did the same. "Ford Hayes was an awkward fellow, rather removed really. Liked but, how should I say this, different. He was a rather good student and did well each year as far as grades were concerned. He wasn't really athletic but managed to play on a few teams in his early years at school. That was during the war and a lot of boys were off overseas. There wasn't much competition." Frank tried to decipher everything he said because he knew it was only the veil of truth, a veneer. So far he figured that Hayes must have been some all-around kid. Smart and athletic. But what did awkward mean, removed? Richard must have hated him.

Richard continued. "He came from a rather wealthy family and didn't want for much. It is always that sort of family that creates fellows like Hayes, not like those of us who had to make a struggle of it." Richard finished his glass. "He seemed to have it all until the day he was thrown out of school." Richard got up to get more whiskey. Frank took a sip of his. He held himself steady and concentrated on the whiskey. What the fuck kind of struggle did Richard ever experience? Willie would always tell him that it was a matter of perspective. One man's paradise is another man's hell. Frank wanted to be diplomatic. He also wasn't willing to give Richard more of his energy than was necessary. He decided to continue talking about Hayes. At least it was better than talking about Richard.

"Why did he get thrown out?" Frank asked, measuring each word as he sometimes felt he had to with people such as Richard for fear of having his grammar or verb tense or some other thing corrected.

"Well," he said, thinking for a moment, "I forget what he did. He didn't get caught changing test scores in the Master's notebooks like your good friend Stone. Rather, it was something more radical and perverse." And probably far less petty, thought Frank.

"He made a scene of some sort, I forget now. I think..." Richard was interrupted by the sound of laughter coming from the kitchen. Frank and Richard looked and saw the door swing open and Willie and her aunt come out, each with a tray. Willie had the dessert and Trish a pot of coffee and cups.

"Trish darling," said Richard, "why did Ford get thrown out of the College?"

"College," said Willie, rolling her eyes, "is that what you old boys talk about all the time. College. How dull, I'm sorry, Frank," she said putting the tray down on the coffee table.

"No, no. I asked Richard about Hayes. He was just filling me in," said Frank.

"That's right, Willie. So, none of the barrister's lip from you, young lady," Richard said, looking at her in that sly way, that Frank had grown to dislike very quickly.

"Trish darling," said Richard, "why did Hayes get tossed

out of the school? I think Frank here is doing a piece for his tabloid."

Willie's eyes met Frank's and they exchanged unsaid sympathies.

Trish rolled her eyes in a way that almost summed up her entire philosophy of life. "Oh, Ford was causing another scene so they threw him out. He was a very dramatic person, very dramatic. It was bothersome to his family and everyone around him, extremely bothersome." Trish began cutting cake and placing the pieces on plates. "My good Lord, I mean, what about the whole incident in law school," she said as she passed a piece to Frank. "He didn't want to go to law school so he ran away from home, just ran away." She passed a piece to Richard.

"Well, I hardly call disappearing for a year and a half running away from home, Trish," said Richard. She was only half-listening as she passed a piece of cake to Willie and then served herself. "Well, it was still a mean thing to do," she said pouring coffee into cups.

"What do you mean, disappeared?" asked Frank. He was becoming more intrigued by Hayes.

"He left one day," said Richard. "And he wasn't heard from again for a year and a half – when he simply reappeared." For some reason, looking at Richard, that seemed logical to Frank.

Trish changed the subject with a wave and began talking about Willie's job, trying to impress Richard. She seemed to have accomplished her mission. Richard shook his head as the list of names of large corporations and well-known business figures were recited. Frank sat and listened and drank his coffee, realizing that for Trish, talking about the past was supposed to be pleasant, and the topic of Cecil Rutherford Hayes wasn't.

Chapter 2

"I did not say that...no...noooo...no way, forget it," Frank looked over at Jane. She was screaming into the phone. Her free arm was flailing like an albatross trying to take off.

"You, my friend, and please take this with the intention it is meant, are crazy, absolutely crazy, if you think that I am not going to print every Goddamn word of that interview...now is not... No way...forget it...now is not the time to retract anything...listen we're close to filing..." Jane paused for a moment and looked at Frank. She rolled her eyes and smiled.

"I don't care, you should have thought about that yesterday when you had your fucking chance." Pause. "Fuck you," she said, her voice now calm. "What?...what?...when?...ok...o-k, o-k, fifteen minutes but it had better be good and you are definitely paying."

She looked at the phone as though she were about to slam it down. Then, noticing that Frank was looking, she put it down gently. Jane Simons was at the desk next to Frank's. She was fifty-two and had been a columnist since the late eighties. Frank had wondered if Carl, the city editor and his direct boss, had put him beside Jane to help calm him into the job or scare him out of it. She always seemed flustered, flattening her wire-like grey hair constantly. Every time she pushed it down, it bounced back up. Useless. She was a tall thin woman. Her eyes were blank and intense at the same time. She wore a patterned dress with thin straps over the shoulders. Her arms were remarkably thin and the skin had a warm dark tan. Frank thought her attractive but wasn't sure about her emotional state. She had been away the first week he had moved to his new desk. Now, between phone calls, she was trying to make him feel at home on his new side of the journalistic world.

"So, you got tired of beat reporting, hey, well, we'll fix you up around here. Read that thing you did last year on the city waste disposal thing, great stuff, really great stuff, had it magnetted to my fridge for about a month. I'd get up early every garbage day to try and catch those fucking bastards but never got them." She smiled. A pen still dangled from her mouth like a cigarette. He couldn't help but look around his desk for an ashtray.

"Well," she continued, "how are things otherwise, you comfortable and all that, Carl put you in the right place? If you've got any questions, well, feel free, feel free...oh shit," she looked at her watch and then grabbed her purse, which hung from her chair. "I gotta go, see ya." She turned and walked away. It was obvious that Jane also wondered why Carl had put him beside her on his first day. Frank took her ranting as some sort of pep talk.

Steven Hunt threw himself into Jane's vacated chair. "Mr. Columnist," he said. Steven had a coffee in his hand. He rested it on his ample belly. "How are you feeling?"

"Shitty," said Frank.

"Thought so. How's Jane, she crazy or what? Shit, I had to sit in a car with her for an hour once to cover the prelim down in St. Catherines on the Bernardo case. I was ready to fucking hit the guard rail if she didn't shut up." Steven took a sip of his coffee. Frank and Steven had started together at the paper just after college. Steven had gone to journalism school at the same university where Frank had been editor of the student newspaper. Both were the only two of the twenty-five or so reporters

hired that year who survived the huge layoffs a few years after
Stone had taken over. Steven had the courts beat. They saw a
lot of each other when Frank covered city hall.

"Well, she hasn't made me want to throw anything at her
yet, but I've only been here five minutes."

"Give her time," said Steve, taking another sip of coffee.

"Had breakfast yet?" asked Frank, looking for a reason to
avoid beginning to write.

"Yeah. Anyway, I've got to head down to Provincial today
for a sentencing hearing."

"Which one?" asked Frank.

"Oh, some hit and run thing from over near Danforth and
Pape. You remember, they finally got the guy, after he was hiding up in Kapuskasing for nearly a year."

"On the run for a year, Christ, up in that wilderness,"
Frank said.

"Shit Frank, just because it ain't 'Torana', doesn't mean it's
the wilderness," said Steven, looking Frank straight in the eye.

Frank had forgotten that Steven was from a small town in
northern Ontario.

"Anyway, I should go," he said as he got up and left.

Frank looked around the editorial floor. His desk was off
to the side toward the wall now. He had been moved from the
heart of the room where the day-to-day news was dealt with.
From the centre out, the different news departments formed
circles around where the City Editor and his assistants sat.
Then, moving along in ever-increasing pie-shaped wedges were
the entertainment, sports, national and international news
desks. There were no walls between the rows of desks. Phones
rang constantly and there was the noise of people talking and
keyboards being tapped. How calming that noise had become
to Frank since he first entered the newsroom. At first he had
been somewhat distracted by the sounds that filled the space
around the room. The loud laughter and TV sets and police
scanners seemed everywhere, their sounds painting the room

with a symphony of events and happenings. It was hard work blocking it all out in his first weeks. But once he had gotten used to it, he needed that noise.

Frank's desk was shoved up against the side of the building now, away from the center. His job had changed and with it the need for him to be in the thick of things. The wall, covered with a beige cloth, formed a boundary for his space. Jane used her wall space to tack up small articles from other newspapers and publications. There were some old pictures of her, younger with hair even less controlled, standing beside a tall man in a dark suit. Frank wondered if it was her husband. He was smiling and she was not. It seemed that she was in her mid-twenties. Another photo was of her in a scrum with Trudeau. Trudeau looked very young and judging by the clothes it was perhaps the late seventies. Trudeau smiled at the group of reporters. Jane, like the rest of them, smiled back.

Frank took out his wallet and removed a picture of Willie. He took a pin from his desk drawer and pinned the small photo to the beige wall.

***

Frank got to Dante's a little early and sat at the bar waiting for Willie. He liked Dante's even though it was filled with the after-work crowd from the office towers. It was a dark and simple place tucked neatly away on a side street just north of King and west of University Avenue. There was a mixture of theatre and business people. There wasn't any music blaring to stop conversations. The best part was that every night except Thursday, the crowd thinned out at about ten. By eleven hardly anyone was there and you felt like the place was all yours. Until then, the placed buzzed with action. The noise would get to a fevered pitch and on some nights, when the markets were good or bad, or there was action in the newsrooms around town, the place seemed to be electric. Everyone had the after-effects of watching computers all day. Their brains were on information overload. When they shut their eyes, they could see their screens. And, like the overflow of information that was available to them, they tried to drown each other out as they spoke, hoping that by being louder than the person beside them, their point would be more important. Small groups of men and women yelled at each other.

"No fucking way," barked a boyish-looking man with pudgy cheeks. "No way they'll separate."

"They're gone," said a women in a louder, screeching voice that sounded like a subway train going around the Union Station bend at top speed.

"No way," bellowed the first man. "They'd be crazy, they'd be ruined economically. Why the hell would they want to slit their throats like that?"

"You're right," yelled another man, thin and bony with white skin and a bowl hair cut. "They would be crazy to leave the free trade agreement behind, and if they did leave, we'd fuck them if they tried to get back in."

Frank shook his head. Even in the summer, when the rest of the western world seemed to slow down, at Dante's, there was action. Most of it was business.

Dante's wasn't one of those kitschy places that tried too hard to have atmosphere. It was a bar. There was a European feel to it. The food was interesting and the drinks weren't that expensive by downtown standards. They had a decent house wine, and if you asked for a double, they would bring a large heavy glass for only a dollar more than a single. Frank liked drinking wine out of heavy water glasses. Fancy wine glasses were fine for restaurants, but at a bar he didn't like their feel.

He could remember growing up. His father and mother would have a glass of wine with every meal. His father would make about 40 gallons every year and store it in their cellar. All of his parents' friends had storage cellars. They were always filled with wonderful things. Wine in oak casks, preserves, jams, pickles, beets, peppers, and cabbage. Bags of garlic and potatoes hung from the wall. There were onions and vegetables in the summer. Frank loved being sent down there by his mother to get something that she needed. He would linger and take in the magical smells. After years of pizzas and chicken wings in pubs, he realized that the smell was life, pure and unprocessed.

Willie walked in at the far end of Dante's. Frank saw her and, after trying many times, finally caught her attention. As she walked toward him, men in suits with glasses of good scotch gazed at her from head to toe. She had a business suit on and the hem of her skirt floated just above her knee. She wore no stockings and the tanned muscles of her calves tensed and loosened with each stride. Men turned to follow her motion. At one time, Frank was very jealous of those gazes. He was over that now. He felt, in a small way, proud that they acknowledged her beauty.

She stood beside him and touched his shoulder. He slipped off the seat and let her sit down.

"You look tired," he said to her with a smile.

"I'm exhausted," she said. Frank waved at the bartender and she came over. Willie worked hard at her job. Frank looked at her as she slid her shoes off. Frank thought about his own job. He was young and he had been successful in his profession. Had it been luck? Many of his university friends were more talented and committed than he, and they were unemployed or struggling in jobs they hated. They either had too little experience or they were overqualified. It was hard to see them getting turned down for jobs. It was hard to walk into offices and see them manning phone banks or taking on administrative assistant jobs. It was hard to listen to them talk about going back to school as if it was such a positive step for them when, for the most part, it was the only step they could take. He waved the bartender down.

"What can I get you?" she asked, putting down a cardboard coaster advertising a local brewery.

"I'll have a spritzer," Willie said.

"I'll have another double red and could you bring us a couple of menus, please?" he said.

"So," Willie said, "how'd things go today?"

"Not bad," said Frank. "I struggled for an idea of what to write until about two o'clock, but once it came to me, it flowed out like the warm crap that it was."

Willie bit her lip and frowned. "That's good to hear." Her warm smile helped him feel less depressed.

"Actually, it wasn't that great again today," said Frank emptying his glass of wine. "It wasn't what you could call a great effort."

"Oh, Frank," said Willie in a soft reassuring voice, "That's too bad, what went wrong?"

"I don't know, it's just...I guess it's, well for now anyway, it's just easier to write when the inspiration comes from someplace else, somewhere outside rather than from within me," he said. He found it hard to look at her as he spoke.

"Well, you'll get over that. You know what to do, and you're good at what you do. Just remember that tomorrow when you sit down to write. Remember that you aren't there because of any reason other than you. Be confident."

Frank shrugged. Willie was confident in all things – sometimes too confident. At times he admired her for that. He had never met anyone who was willing to tackle any job like she did. She had inspired him since the day he met her. Even when she fell short as she often did, she took the experience and learned from it rather than let it defeat her.

When the drinks came, Willie took a long sip. Frank looked at her delicate mouth and her high cheekbones. Her body seemed too small for someone her age. It seemed to belong to a child instead of a grown woman. Frank had often wondered how those men in the corporate boardrooms felt when they first met Willie. The men she worked with tended to have a conservative view of things. With that view came a belief that to be powerful one had to look powerful. It was true to this day. Willie didn't look powerful. She looked fragile at times. It wasn't until she began speaking that you realized she was someone to be respected. Unfortunately, sometimes, by that point it was too late. By then, the "big brains," as Willie liked to call them, had already given too much, had asked too little. Their position was lost.

"What happened in the world of corporate robbery today?" asked Frank. She gave him a small smile.

"Same old thing," she said. "Some jerk has gotten himself in trouble with the tax department and now he might have to go to court. All day I listened to him rant about how unfair it is that the taxes are so high and how he created wealth and the government should be thanking him, not penalizing him for making a lot of money and generating wealth for all Canadians. Blah, blah, blah." Willie took another drink.

"Who is this guy?" he asked and then took a drink of his wine.

She looked at him and gave a small laugh. "None of that now, you won't find any information on me," she said.

"Not even if I feel around," he said with a smile.

"Not tonight you won't," she said

"Now, now. What have you got hidden in here?" Frank caressed her thin waist.

"Stop it," she said in a sing-song voice before slapping his hands away playfully.

"Ok, ok, I hear you." Frank took up his drink again.

"Did you have fun this weekend?" she asked.

"Yeah, I did. Too many bug bites, but otherwise it was great," he said.

"Did you like the people?" she asked.

"Well, Jonathan is great and the others are, you know, fine." Frank felt uncomfortable judging her friends. "But what is the deal with the drunk in the cheesy sunglasses?" asked

Frank, "What the hell was his story?"

"Brian is an idiot. He always has been and he always will be." There was a decisive hard tone to her voice that made Frank think she had long ago made up her mind about him.

"You don't have to convince me of that," said Frank.

Willie didn't say any more. Frank could see in her face that there was something to her tone and opinion. He knew her to be a person who would go to great extremes to help people, even people she didn't particularly like. She liked and disliked just as anyone would, but she managed to find some line of thought or act of sensibility in a person that made them whole, no matter how they might treat her. That always let her care for them and she felt better caring for people than not. He tried to snap her out of her brief mood.

"I like Richard, do you think he and Trishie are getting nasty?"

"Frank!" she said, letting out a giggle.

"What, you think Aunt Trish and Dickie aren't...intimate?"

"Are you kidding?" she said, putting the glass to her mouth, "I'm sure of it. I just don't want to think about it." She took a drink.

"What about this Hayes guy? Your family always surprises me," said Frank.

"Which Hayes?" she asked, taking another drink.

"You know, the guy we talked about last night."

"Oh," said Willie, "I don't know much about him, really. He's related to my mother's family and I think my father's as well, through a whole bunch of other people." Her tired eyes told Frank that she wasn't interested in talking or much else.

"Do you want to just go home now and forget dinner?" he said. Willie smiled faintly and stretched her neck to kiss him.

"Okay," She stood up and put her shoes back on.

They walked to her building's garage to get her car. It was a beautiful night. Frank couldn't help but stare up at the tall buildings looking like fluorescent ladders leading to the blue night sky. He tried to distance himself from what went on in those financial towers. He took every opportunity to stay away from the business district around King and Bay. The entire area was a crazed mix of suits, miniskirts and bicycle couriers, all trying to avoid each other as they rushed toward some destination. It was beyond hectic, beyond fast. He could still remember listening to the thousands of feet plodding along the underground walkways. The noise was tremendous and awe-inspiring at the same time. But it was too much for him, getting caught in the flow of people going in one direction while he tried to go in another. Once, he went along a concourse and out the far end of a building simply to avoid the moving mass. What he did like was the way the area looked at night. It was shiny and manicured, almost deserted. It was hard to believe that it was the same place he tried to avoid during the day.

Frank looked at Willie and the day before flashed back as a vibrant blue memory. Her standing on the dock, ready for her swim. The trees and rocks around them. How these two places, the concrete and lights they were now walking through and the sun and water of the day before, could be connected amazed him. Such chaos and calm.

They often called the the business world a "jungle" and Frank would laugh at the metaphor. It was anything but a jungle. It was tame and calculated and safe. Still, looking up at the monuments that it had created for itself, Frank could feel a sense of power. One he wanted to stay away from.

Chapter 3

The next morning Frank got to Murray's early. "Hey Frank!" and "Franko my friend!" greeted him as he came through the door. There they were, sitting where they always sat, wearing what they always wore, drinking coffee, like always. They were the boys, the counter gang.

In university, Frank and his friends would search for the best bar in town, the best cup of coffee, and the best greasy spoon. There was a set of criteria to be met for each. A bar had to have lots of different beers on tap, the music couldn't be too loud, and there should be no lines to get in. A good cup of coffee had to be rich and strong, not the warm coloured water that most places served, and free refills were a must.

A greasy spoon had to have atmosphere. The food didn't have to be good, just lots of it. Big portions were important. But atmosphere was the real key. The seats had to be worked in, perhaps patched with duct tape. The waitresses had to be friendly and learn your name or at least call you "dear" or "honey". And no matter how old they were, they had to flirt with you. And there had to be regulars. People who went there as though it were a church service. They had to have faith in the place and go there, whatever it took, daily. That's who the boys at the counter were. Frank loved Murray's. He'd loved it the first day he walked in.

The boys sat where they always sat, at the counter. They never tipped Sally, or the other waitresses, or Murray or his wife Kim. They were old pressmen who had worked for the paper and retired some years before. They were pensioned men with no hobbies. They were lost the day after they were given their gold watches. All they knew and all they had ever known was work, hard work. The day they had to stop working was, for them, the day they had no idea of what to do next. Without anything else to do, they still woke up early each morning, showered, shaved, put on a hat and tie, and headed down to Murray's for breakfast. In this ritual they found some purpose.

At Murray's they were like a group of judges ready to discuss and give verdicts on cases one after another. Every topic and every opinion was measured against all things that came before. They would throw insults around, calling each other a liar every time a precious fact was misspoken or treated without the due reference. Then with every verdict they would slam down their coffee cups like gavels on a judge's bench. BAM! BAM! Frank wondered how they didn't manage to break those cups. Murray must have bought some sort of extra durable china.

"Hello fellas, how the hell are you?" Frank called out in a loud boisterous tone that sounded like a male Katherine Hepburn.

"Hey Franko," said Murray, wiping up some spilled cream on the counter. "Breakfast today?"

"Just coffee," Frank said emphasizing the last line.

"Health nut," said Murray with a smile. Murray didn't say much but when he did, it was always a jab.

"Hey Frank," Charlie Jones yelled, even though he sat at the counter directly in front of him. "Hear you've given up honest work."

Hank Simpson, sitting right beside Charlie as he always

did, joined in. "What's he up to?" he said with mock interest. "Running the flower show beat?" Frank smiled.

"Are you kidding?" Charlie yelled even louder, "he couldn't handle the flower show beat, that's real reporting. Nope, Franko's hit the big time, he's a *col-hume-nista*," said Charlie, drawing out the name. The counter exploded with laughter and the sound of grown men acting like schoolboys watching a fight. Frank laughed. The noise continued.

"How you gonna save the world today, Frank?" asked Charlie.

"He's gonna tell everyone just what he thinks," said Hank.

"Oh shit, better move back to Montreal and vote Yes." The counter exploded with laughter and the cups hit the table. BAM! BAM!

Sally, Murray's only morning waitress, had a wide smile on her face when she brought Frank his coffee. Frank smiled back and grabbed the newspaper left on the table beside him. It was *The Globe and Mail*. Grey and serious, it was a competing paper favoured by those interested in business, national and international affairs all with a slant toward business interests. Frank had never even seen a copy of it until university.

He skimmed over the reports about politics on Parliament Hill and business on Bay Street and read a story about his parents' home country. There was still fighting going on. He thought about his huge family there, people he barely knew but who looked like him and had the same features and mannerisms. Luckily, they were away from the majority of the war, but close enough. He had turned down that job. He was certainly qualified for the assignment. The language was second nature to him and he knew the territory. But the idea of exploiting his own relatives to make a name for himself didn't appeal to him. It had made him think for the first time that a lot of the international reporting was really about chasing conflict and trying desperately to serve the reporter's interest and nothing else. Most of the news that came back meant nothing to the people who read it. Some might talk about it at a dinner party or send some dollars for relief funds. Others might change investment strategies or cancel planned trips, but these things never really affected the people who read *The Globe.*

Frank finished the last of his coffee and put the main section of the paper down. At the front of the Sport section was another story about money and athletes. Money, thought Frank. The Arts section was touting another author with a book that shocked the country to the core. Goddamned authors, thought Frank. At the top of a section called Leisure was a story about a group that was trying to open up more land for cottages. The picture had a mid-thirty-ish couple in business attire frowning at the high cost of summer homes on the lakes around Georgian Bay. They were holding out a map with huge red areas marked as crown land.

Fucking incredible, he thought.

"More coffee?" said Sally, holding a fresh pot.

"Always Sally, you know that," he said.

Frank returned to the paper. He turned to the Op/Ed page and looked for something interesting. Nothing. Two pieces about Bosnia by Canadian historians. There was an editorial on how the areas just north of the city had to be opened up for more industry, resource based business, and to allow an expanding Toronto population more access to recreation or the present facilities would be overburdened. The other editorial talked about The Bank of Canada policy and how it was hurting Canada in its attempt to compete on a global market. "Crap!" he said and put down the paper. "Fucking accountants write this thing," he said.

"Those were the same accounts that laid me off," said someone at the counter and a murmur of laughter followed. Frank put down the paper and decided to head to the office to see if he couldn't come up with something better than what he had just read.

***

"Listen, you little prick, I don't give a shit if you get fired," Jane was wooing a source again. "You know what, I'll get you fired and then I'll spread your Goddamn name all over town so that you'll never get hired again and...what, what did you call me... Listen you little fly, my column is read by half a million people a day, that is a five with five little zeros like you beside it, you shithead." Jane stopped, letting that fact float over the telephone line. Frank thought he could hear the lines crackle.

"A drink? What fucking time is it? 10:45, oh, is it that late? Okay, I'll meet you but remember, don't try any of that shit on me, and keep your hands to yourself this time. And you're buying." She looked at the computer screen in front of her. Her fingers pounded on the keyboard.

"Oh, hi Jane," Steven Hunt stood in front of her desk. He spoke to her in a bored, yawning tone. "It's 11 a.m. you know," he said to her. Jane looked at him for a second.

"Shit, I've got an appointment," she said. She bolted from her chair and grabbed her purse. It didn't come off right away and she dragged the chair behind her for a couple of feet until she managed to free the bag. Steven walked over to the chair and wheeled it to the desk. He sat down.

"Another day, another disaster," said Steven. He didn't hide the fact that Frank's column wasn't very good.

"It was a piece of shit wasn't it, Steve?" Frank asked, knowing the answer.

"Well," said Steven, shrugging.

"Steve, I haven't got anything to say," confessed Frank.

"Don't worry about saying anything. Just piss someone off. It's the easiest way. That's what Jane does. She is pissing people off everyday of the week. It's her career." Steven looked down at her desk. He shook his head at the mess. There were clippings from magazines, empty coffee cups, bags from the deli on the building's main floor, a date book that lay open but had nothing written in it. There were a couple of copies of yesterday's paper, both turned to her column. Unopened letters were everywhere. Steven picked one up. He waved it at Frank.

"Every day she sits here and decides to piss someone off. And why?" There was silence for a moment. Steven threw the letter back on the desk. Frank had always thought Steven was a thinker. He was by far the brightest young reporter at the paper. He had won every award that was available at his journalism school and had a job waiting for him at three different papers. It was surprising even to Frank that Steven had been passed over for the columnist's job. He was the new breed of journalist. Well-educated and cynical at an early age. Jane was from the old school. She had been an idealist once. She had wanted to change the world. Now, all that was left for her was controversy and scandal. They were the building blocks of fame in their profession.

Steven waved his hand casually toward the window in the newsroom. "They want something to react to. Without it, they couldn't function." Steven looked at the computer screen. He touched the bottom of it.

"They need her and she needs them. She gives them stimulus and they think they have opinions. It's a beautiful relationship, like the one you had with Rachel at school, remember? You'd see each other at a bar, fight all night, go home, screw your brains out and then wake up in the morning satisfied and embarrassed, swearing it would never happen again."

"Jane wasn't always like that, you know." Steven turned his head up to the ceiling. "I guess nobody starts off a defeated drunk. That just kind of creeps up on you in those moments of self-importance when you start to believe the perception rather than the reality."

Steven moved his hand around the sleek computer, the crackling box of chips and wires and power. He felt the lower unit. His hands were gentle and soft on the cold plastic. He reached for the switch at the back and clicked it off. The screen, full of type, disappeared. Laughing, Steven stood up and walked away.

Eventually, Frank managed to bang out his necessary amount of words about what to do with the city's vacant waterfront property. It was an old issue. He tried to add a fresh angle but it was no use.

He filed his copy in the directory for his page on the main server and left a hard copy, in column format, on Carl's desk. He tried to do that without Carl seeing him so that he wouldn't have to tell him in person what he was writing about. It didn't work. Carl always knew what was going on in the newsroom, especially around the three o'clock editorial meeting. He saw Frank put the copy on his desk and walked over.

"How'd it go today?" he asked. There may have been concern in his voice, but Frank wasn't sure. He just might be paranoid.

"Slow."

That was the problem with print. Everything was on record forever. It would be on kitchen tables and desks in dens all over town. People would stuff it in recycling boxes or take it to the cottage where, maybe in two years, using a sheet of newsprint to help start a fire they would see Frank's column and say what a piece of shit it was. Carl didn't like letting crap get printed, but he had no choice with the columnists. Whatever they wrote got in almost without fail.

The subway ride home wasn't long, but some days Frank couldn't help himself and he would doze off. Since he was on the train by seven to get to work and three-thirty to get home, he generally missed the rush hour. Now, he sat in the corner of an almost deserted car. It was one of the older trains. Large padded seats and no air conditioning.

He leaned back and closed his eyes. The stress of the day, his inability to do his job, and the fact that everyone in the newsroom knew it, had zapped him of energy. The seat felt comfortable to his tired body. The rocking of the train helped to relax him. He crossed his arms on his chest. He felt his head nod and caught it. He opened his eyes and looked around him. He closed them again and let his head fall to his chest. Soon, he was sleeping. The dreams came then, filled with the sounds around him. Carl speaking to him, his big bald head. Suddenly Carl began crying in a high-pitched whine. The train lurched and Frank's head shot up. Standing by the door, a young father had his baby in a front carry sack. The baby was crying. The train stopped and the father and child got off.

Frank leaned his head back again. Soon he saw Willie. She was naked, standing on the balcony of her apartment. Her belly was getting bigger. The embryo within was speaking to Frank as Willie looked at him and smiled. The train squealed to a stop and again Frank was awake. He rubbed his face and checked for drool. There was none. He shifted in his seat and looked to see if anyone was watching him. The car was still nearly empty. The train started again and Frank closed his eyes. The dreams were enticing and though the visions were strange, they were pleasant.

His eyes closed again and he was at the lake. He sat on a dock like the one at Jonathan's, the water calm around him. Ripples began to form and increased in size. It became rough. Soon large waves pounded the dock. The wood around him began to collapse. He stood and tried to make for the shore but when he turned the shore was gone. He was standing in the middle of the lake, the dock breaking up around him. He was in the water and he was sinking. The weight of his clothing pulled him down. He tried to keep his head above the water but he couldn't. Soon only his hands were above water, thrashing around, reaching. A hand, filled with strength, took his and with one great motion pulled him onto shore. Frank saw that it was the hand of an old man, spotted and wrinkled, but strong. His eyes followed the arm up to the shoulder until he looked at the face. It was the old man from the lake, the one he had seen from the dock. It was him.

Frank woke up. The train was stopped at a station. He looked around and tried to get his bearings. An elderly lady was sitting across from him. When he looked at her she smiled meekly. He rubbed his eyes and looked at the name of the station. For some reason he could not make out the word. R-O-S-E-D-A-L-E. He looked at it, not taking his eyes from it. Then it hit him. Rosedale, he was at Rosedale Station. He sat up straight in his seat and looked at the elderly lady. She looked at him and smiled again. He looked back and smiled. Frank stayed awake until Lawrence Station and then got off. Instead of waiting for the bus, he walked.

Magnetic North

Chapter 4

The next morning was another hot August day in Toronto. It was muggy and a mist seemed to hang over the city. Frank walked to the office from the subway, looking up at the buildings that were like huge trees in a forest of concrete. How the day and the night could bring such different perspectives on the exact same spot. He thought that at one point there were probably real trees on the very spot where these huge granite towers stood. Trees like the ones they had seen the past weekend. Thinking of the weekend made him think of Hayes.

Usually he didn't become intrigued by Willie's family no matter how interesting they thought they were. She had ambassadors and politicians in the family. Her great uncle had been a cabinet minister. People related to her regularly showed up in the paper for one thing or another. Some parks in the city had the family name on them. There were buildings at the university, he remembered taking classes at them. He had often wondered who the people were whose names appeared on the buildings. When he was younger, he felt they must have been heroes. People who had done some great good and society had decided to honour them with a building or a road. He soon learned that wasn't always the case.

He thought of the owner of the paper, Harold Stone. While most men his age were retiring, Stone ran one of the world's largest media organizations. Although Frank had never met him, he was ultimately the man who made the final decision. There was no mistake about it. Stone had come from money. Lots of it. He was born into a prominent family in a small and wealthy country. From the fortune his father left him, he made an even larger fortune. But that wasn't the story Stone wrote in his autobiography. Frank remembered the first page.

Life for me as a child, the book began, *was one of hardship and loss. Unsure of our family's position in the world, I remember crying at night, wondering if there would be bread on our table in the morning.* What bullshit. Frank couldn't help but let out a small indignant laugh about the whole thing. He was often amazed by the self-inflated history of people. How small problems became enormous hardships. People like Stone had managed to turn life and its living into some sort of epic journey, a war to be fought, a demon to conquer. But the epic journey was for themselves only. Those around them, those of little significance, lived lives that were meaningless. And, as if by divine providence, these epic heroes seemed always to arrive, always to defeat, always to win. Because they were the victors of this war, the only one they ever fought, the war of wealth and power and greed, a war whose victory was handed to them on a silver platter, they wrote the history. That history was always kind to their past. Too kind.

Hayes had had it all as well. And he left. Where did he go? Why? The days that Frank would spend when he was younger dreaming about what he would do "if". He had played the game, his friends had played it, his parents, everyone he knew. What if...I won the lottery? First I would... What if I had three wishes? What if, what if? Everyone filled in their own blanks. As Frank grew older he began to realize that some of those blanks are filled in for you. Life has a way of sending you down a road that is in keeping with where your journey starts. It isn't often you can stray from what seems like a straight line to your eventual destination. The inertia can seem too much. Hayes should have been dragged through his life, unaware of why, only knowing that it all seemed familiar. The conversations and the people and the houses, the streets, the smells and the life.

Instead, Hayes stepped outside that world, a world many aspired to, dreamed of being able to live within. On his way to the rest of his life, inside that life he took a turn so enormous, he wasn't seen again for eighteen months. Was it really strange?

He realized that he was walking very quickly. He was almost running.

***

Frank turned on his computer. He heard the whirr of the fan in the hard drive and the *ping* of the screen as it warmed up. The screen came to its full-colour brightness. Launching his date book program, he called up the day's date and looked to see what was on. Nothing. Completely empty. No appointment and worse yet, no column ideas. It was true that not everyone was cut out to do every job. The newsroom was filled with reporters who hadn't been able to become editors, columnists, or whatever. Frank had thought it would be easy. He was quickly realizing that it wasn't.

Frank looked around the room to see if Carl was on the floor. No sign of him. He took a sip of coffee. Maybe he should try calling one of his old contacts down at city hall. Frank picked up the phone and dialed the number.

"Councilman Kawaja's office," came a woman's voice on the other end of the line.

"Hi Mary," Frank said with familiarity, "this is Frank Medved at the..." Before he could get out his greeting, the councilman's secretary was already trying to get rid of him.

"Frank, he's in a meeting right now. Do you want to leave a message? He should be back soon. Flaherty from Etobicoke is going to be hogging the floor today so he doesn't want to stay too long," she said.

"Flaherty is still up to his old crap isn't he?" Asked Frank.

"Mm hmm," hummed the secretary.

"Just get him to call me when he gets in, would you?"

"Sure, Frank," she said. They both said goodbye and Frank hung up the receiver. He thought about his time at city hall. It was messy business down there, but as they say, all politics are local and local politics was the lifeblood of the political system. Frank loved it.

Since he couldn't talk to Kawaja yet, he played the great media game. He began to wait. Most reporting, like most research of any kind, is a lot of waiting. You have to wait and then you have to dig. It wasn't the life people thought it was. Frank remembered teaching a night class at the university's journalism program. The students came in wide-eyed. They wanted to be reporters but they didn't know why. Worse, they didn't know what they wanted to report on. A lot of them just wanted to be in the know, or gain access to people and events and places that few other professions were allowed. Sports reporters wanted to hang out with athletes. Political types wanted to hang out with politicians. Some just wanted to see themselves on TV or be recognized the way media personalities are, at a local restaurant or grocery store. They wanted people to nudge other people and say, "Hey isn't that the girl from the news?" Frank would try to tell them that it was a lot of work and that it wasn't really worth the rewards. Something else had to motivate you.

Frank put his pointer back onto the screen's menu and scrolled down to launch his data link program. He wondered about his conversation with Richard. Thrown out of school, that isn't any small matter. If your parents pay the money required to place you in a school like that, they have to have good reason to kick you out. Hayes. The name sounded too familiar now. Hayes Street, off Jarvis Street. The Hayes Wing at Queen's Park. Hayes Park near King and Church. The Hayes Mansion that the children's hospital used as a residence for out-of-town patients and their families. Frank pictured the name everywhere.

"I've got some time," he said to himself, "let's see about this Hayes guy."

The database was linked directly into the files of the newspaper. Once the responsibility of a team of librarians at the newspaper, the archives were now all electronically kept in a central computer. The input was easy, all the stories were written on computers. Freelance stories were only accepted if they came in on diskette. What had taken a group of people a week to accomplish now took one computer person about half a day. Every story ever published in the paper was on file. You could also access almost every other daily newspaper in Canada, as well as international papers such as *The London Times* or *The New York Times*. It was all at his fingertips. Information was readily available, if you had the money to pay for it.

Frank went to the search screen and selected a name search.

"Hayes, Cecil R," he said aloud as he typed. He pressed enter.

Using powerful mainframes, these searches usually took a matter of seconds. That was what the paper had set up. It was a time-saving measure. Get the people on and off the system quickly. Get them to writing or digging further. It was the right idea in Frank's mind. Less time waiting and more time getting the story written.

Frank seemed to be waiting longer than necessary and that concerned him. It had been almost ten minutes, an eternity by computer standards. The patterns of the screen saver kept fluxing from one shape to another, hypnotically. He grew tired of watching it. He turned away and looked to see if Carl was around. He wasn't. Frank returned to the screen. The motion of the patterns was wave-like. Then, suddenly, the search screen was again visible. A prompt read, "Your search has matched 1442 files."

"Holy shit," Frank said aloud. "What the..." The amount was enormous for a search that was so closely defined. For a person who wasn't the mayor, or a premier, or the prime minister or a sports or entertainment figure, the number was incredible.

"Who the hell is this guy?" said Frank to himself.

Now the question was where to begin. He had to redefine his search.

Frank thought of the conversation from the night before. Hayes had disappeared at some point. He would start with that. This man had disappeared twice. The earlier disappearance was where he would begin. Frank typed into the screen, "Hayes, Cecil Rutherford, Missing, 1940s". Frank thought for a moment. Was this worthwhile? He knew nothing about Hayes. Why bother? He had a feeling that once he pressed the return key he wouldn't be able to stop himself. Did he have the time? It was someone from Willie's crazy family, after all. They all had a knack for getting into the paper for ridiculous things. So what if this one managed to inflate his own ego to a huge proportion? Why should Frank care? Then he thought back to the train ride home. There was Hayes in his dream, or so he thought. Frank didn't much believe in the idea of dreams having meaning. He liked proof, he needed tangible evidence, something he could touch, a criminal they could put away. He didn't want this thing to begin because of a dream. "What thing?" He thought to himself. "There isn't anything here."

Frank rubbed his eyes and searched his desk for his coffee. Things hadn't been going well in his new job and now he was trying to decide whether to take a couple of hours of the paper's time to satisfy his own curiosity. He took a sip of coffee. He looked around for Carl. He couldn't see him. He took another long sip of coffee and imagined it was scotch. He held it in his mouth, savored the flavour, then swallowed hard as though it gave the sting of liquor. He contorted his face. He looked at the enter key on his keyboard. He put his right index finger on it gently, then softly pushed. The screen went into search mode and a small watch appeared showing that the search was working. He finished the last of his coffee and put his cup on the end of his desk. The computer went dark as the screen saver came on.

"Come on," he said out loud. He looked around again in search of Carl. No sign of him. The screen popped back on again. There were only twelve matches to his search. "Great," he said. Frank quickly scanned the headlines provided. The stories were listed in chronological order. The first headline told the tale. *Son of Prominent Insurance Executive Gone Missing.* Frank selected the first item and pressed enter. The story quickly popped up.

It was reported last evening that Cecil Rutherford Hayes Jr., son of Monarch Insurance Chief Executive Cecil Rutherford Hayes, went missing. The boy was last seen on his way to the University of Toronto Law school by his mother Cresseda Victoria Hayes early that morning. The Hayes family live on a quiet residential street in Rosedale and the boy had decided to walk to what would have been his first day of classes at law school.

Described as a quiet young man, he was already acclaimed as an author in literary circles for a novel and two books of poetry he wrote as an undergraduate at the University. Having given up the literary career for one in law, he was leaving behind what might have been an extraordinary career as a writer.

Police have not yet discovered any clues to the disappearance of Mr. Hayes Jr., but foul play has not yet been ruled out. Police have reported that Mr. Hayes' textbooks were returned to the University of Toronto Bookstore. No clerk at the bookstore remembers seeing who left the books and no refund was given out. The books were identified by the name, C.R. Hayes, imprinted on the inside cover.

The Hayes family are not speaking with the press at this time but wish it known that there is a substantial reward for anyone with information leading to the discovery of their son's whereabouts. Reported by John Franklin Carlisle.

Shit. John Franklin Carlisle. Frank thought for a moment. John Carlisle was Executive Editor of Frank's paper.

He read the other headlines. *Hayes Son Still Missing, Hayes Son Presumed to be Dead, Hayes Family Has Ceremony in Memory of Lost Son.* The dates jumped at that point to a little over a year and a half later. The first headline simply stated, *Hayes Returns,* and then *Hayes Son Walks Into Home as Though Nothing Happened.* And then some odd headlines appeared: *Hayes Book Controversial, Hayes Night on Town Turns Ugly.* Frank quickly scrolled down to find the final few headlines. There were three of them that marked the last of Hayes in the public eye. *Hayes Missing Again, Prominent Family Loses Son Again, Hayes Family Fear: He Will Not be Returning This Time.*

Frank felt a large hand on his back and knew immediately that it was Carl.

"What have you got today?" he asked, leaning down to look at Frank's computer screen.

"Just looking into some stuff," said Frank thinking of how to divert Carl from his search.

"Frank, are you digging up ancient history?" said Carl, sounding surprised. "What the hell is this Hayes crap?"

Carl seemed a little uncomfortable. Frank had never seen him like that before. "Does this inquiry bother you?" asked Frank; it was a standard line for those uneasy with his investigations.

Carl's eyes narrowed. "Cut the crap, Frank." Frank felt the point that Carl was making in his usual blunt way.

"It's just Willie's family, he's an old relative so I thought..." Carl didn't let him finish. He walked away. Frank watched him go. He walked down the hall and toward the door at the back of the editorial floor that led up to the executive offices. Where the hell was he going? I'm screwed, he thought. That's it for being a columnist. It was back to the city hall beat.

He looked at the screen again. His pulse was racing. Carl had shaken him. He had never seen him so upset. Not even the day that he had listened to Mary Streeter and they went with the lead about how the Liberals would stay in Queen's Park until the end of their term on the front cover, only to go to a press conference the next day and find out that Peterson was calling an election two years before the end of his mandate. Shit, in comparison, he barely blinked when that happened. There was also the time that Bill Crouch wrote in his column that the Prime Minister was taking direct payment from a major American firm in the form of advanced salary, to get the free trade deal through. That lawsuit nearly brought the fucking paper down. Carl laughed with Crouch about the whole thing. Why was he so upset about Frank looking into a couple of back news items while he was waiting for a phone call? Frank couldn't help himself; he hit the escape button and went to the item screen and selected the second piece.

The Toronto Police Department has reported no news regarding the disappearance on Tuesday of Cecil Rutherford Hayes Jr., son of Cecil Rutherford Hayes, insurance executive. The mystery surrounding the event has police baffled. The lack of any type of ransom note to this day dismisses the idea that Mr. Hayes Jr. was kidnapped for the purpose of holding him as a hostage in hopes of receiving money from the wealthy insurance executive. The Hayes' one of Toronto's most prominent families...

Frank went back to the headlines. He passed by the next stories and assumed they were updates of the situation. He went to the final selection, dated nearly a year after the first story was published. He looked for Carl as the story appeared onscreen. Just as it came up, he saw Carl walk down the steps. He quickly typed in the code for the screen to print and then quit the program. Carl walked toward him. He didn't like the look on his face. Ah well, Frank thought to himself. If you don't get fired once in this business you're probably not doing something right. Frank's phone rang. He grabbed the handpiece before the first electronic tone could end.

"Frank Medved," he said, putting the receiver between his ear and his shoulder.

"Frank, that you," said a worried voice on the other end of the line.

"Councillor?" said Frank with a confident tone to his voice, "are you free today for lunch?" There was a delay on the other end as the councillor mumbled to himself. Carl got to his desk and Frank held up a finger.

"Sure Frank. What's this about? Are you trying to get something out of me about that rail lands problem? Because if you are, forget it."

"Furthest thing from my mind. I'll see you at Murray's at 1 p.m."

"All right, but you're buying."

"Sure thing."

Frank hung up and spoke before Carl had a chance to.

"I'm meeting with Councillor Kawaja. He's going to give me something about this rail lands deal."

Carl expression changed quickly to its regular placid state.

"Good. What have you got on it?" he asked. Frank was shocked at the change in Carl. Why did this idea bring him back to his old self? The rail lands had been a long-standing issue on the council. It was a dog of a column. One that had been written and rewritten. Frank thought it was strange but he was in no position to analyze.

"Not much right now but he's got something new I think. Could be a development deal finally coming through, something about Olympic Games funding and what would happen. I'll have to see." With that, Frank got up and put on his jacket. Carl took him by the elbow.

"Sorry about before, but I..." he hesitated. Another surprise. Carl always knew what to say and when to say it. "I'm just a little worried about you. You've had a bit of a rocky start."

"Thanks Carl," said Frank. Carl's behaviour didn't make much sense, but he let it go. Frank smiled at him and left. On his way out, he went to the laser printer and picked up the pages.

Frank got to Murray's about 12:30. No booths were available, so he sat at the counter. Murray was there with a coffee before Frank had a chance to get settled.

"Hey Murray," said Frank.

"What's up, Frank?" asked Murray. "You look like hell."

"Don't ask, I don't want to relive it."

"That bad, eh? Well, what can I get you?"

"Nothing right now. I'm waiting for someone. Keep an eye open for a table for me, would you?"

"Next one is yours," said Murray, walking up to the register.

Frank took the pages out of his pocket. He went to the last page and checked the by line. It was Carlisle again. He must have been on this for the whole time. Frank turned to the first page and read the story. Hayes, it seems, just showed up one day at the front door. The maid saw him first and fainted. His mother heard the woman fall and knock over a lamp, came into the front hall, and saw her son standing there, thin and with a smile on his face. She also collapsed. Hayes rushed over, helped her to the sofa, and then did the same for the maid.

"I'm surprised it didn't kill her," said Frank aloud. He took a sip of coffee and read on. Hayes' father was called at his office and told the news. He expressed his happiness and, the story says, met with him later that day.

"Shit, he couldn't take the fucking day off?" said Frank.

Frank felt a hand on his shoulder. The councillor was early, he thought. He turned and saw Carl standing behind him.

"Hey Frank," said the editor in his low smoky voice.

"What the hell are you doing here, Carl?" Frank asked, utterly surprised. Carl never left the building until the paper was put to bed. He was famous for it. He would stay until the last word was set. He would sometimes eat in the cafeteria but usually he grabbed a sandwich and brought it back to his desk. Frank became worried. Was he really in trouble? Murray came over.

"Estelle's got a table for you," he pointed to the waitress cleaning away dishes from a table near the back.

"Let's have a seat," said Carl. Frank was almost too shocked to move. He followed Carl to the back of the restaurant and sat opposite him in the booth.

"Frank, I'm going to be straight with you." Frank heard it in Carl's voice. Could he be there to fire him? Frank quickly went over his options. He could freelance for a while, maybe become a stringer with Canadian Press. "I chewed you out today. I'm sorry." Carl always spoke in edited sentences, saying only what needed to be said.

"Sure," said Frank. He was numb; he had never been fired before. It felt like he was about to have something amputated. He thought he might be sick.

"That Hayes stuff took me by surprise."

Frank tried to shake himself out of his anesthesia. "Look, Carl, it was only a little thing I was doing for Willie's family."

Carl shook his head. "It's been a long time since I've seen that name. When I saw you looking into it..." Carl let the sentence break off.

Frank looked blankly at Carl. He wasn't sure what Carl was talking about but he knew he wasn't being fired. Frank had always liked Carl. If you needed an honest opinion – whether you thought so or not – Carl would provide it. He was a tall, balding scruffy man who wasn't much of a dresser. Brown shoes and pants with a white shirt, and a tie hanging loosely around his neck. It was comforting for Frank to see Carl when he came to the office. He wasn't like the majority of people who worked at the paper. They were a little more wordy, a little more pampered and a lot less real.

He played back Carl's words. Why would that name throw him? A feeble "What?" was all he could manage.

"People don't realize, young people like yourself, that newspapers aren't public service organizations. They aren't there for the good of mankind like so many people would like to think. Years ago that was definitely true. You had papers, lots of them, delivering their news, their way. The truth had little to do with it."

Frank nodded. He didn't interrupt Carl but he didn't know where he was going with his story.

"Most of the old ways, if I can call them that, are gone. Only a few traditions remain. Every paper has them. One at our paper is there are to be no stories about Hayes."

That was why Carl had left his post and come to seek him out. This wasn't about his job. This wasn't about giving a lesson on the history of journalism, this was about Hayes. Who the hell was this Hayes that, years after anyone spoke about him, he could shake the editor of one of Canada's largest newspapers?

"You see, Frank, Hayes was a strange character back forty years ago. I was just a young kid at the time, seventeen or eighteen. I was working at a radio station, helping with the news. That's when Hayes happened. Rich kid from Rosedale disappears. Big deal. So what? His father had practically run the city with a few of his friends. He was more than an insurance executive. He was a big name. And Hayes Jr. was well known in literary circles. He was already an author. More than that, he was on his way to law school and a big future. The way the country was going after the war, he looked sure to make himself a very wealthy man, wealthier than his father. Then he's gone." Carl ended abruptly, much like how the Hayes story must have begun.

Frank nodded yes. Carl continued.

"The kid shows up again about eighteen months later. One day he walks into his family's house wearing the same clothes he was wearing when he went missing. He almost kills his mother. She's hospitalized. Again, lots of stories, but Hayes isn't talking. He refuses to tell anyone where he was or what he did. His father's mad as hell because of it. But what can he do? He's also happy that his son has returned."

Frank couldn't help himself and broke in. "Where did he go?"

"He never told anyone. When everyone thought he had died, all the copies of his books sold out in the stores. They reprinted two more times. He was a national bestseller. The literary world welcomed him back as a celebrity. He made a lot of money from the royalties. For the next few years he's all over the paper. He's at every event that the city has. Always in his tuxedo. But he isn't much liked by that crowd. He's always getting into battles over something or other. He got into a fight at an Empire Club luncheon. He was arrested more than once for disturbing the peace. There are rumours about him and different women, some of them married. He becomes a real pain in the ass for a certain crowd of elites. I don't have to tell you that Carlisle was a member of that group. So was Stone." There was a silence as that name lingered.

"And at the same time, Hayes is writing these books that are scathing accounts about life in Toronto. By the end of it, he's pretty much hated by the whole lot of them. Including our friend, the editor."

"Shit," Frank took mental notes, trying to piece together the man.

"One day while on a fishing trip, he disappears without a trace. The guy is gone again. He's in a plane with some pilot, going to fish in some remote area. The plane never returns. It's in the fall, so they put on a big search because they figure it might snow at any time. They search for about two weeks and then they have the biggest first snowfall in history. Almost two feet. They give up. Some think that it might be another hoax but there is a pilot with him. The feeling is that he is dead for sure.

"Right after Hayes disappeared for the second time, Carlisle became an editor. There is still tremendous interest in the Hayes story. When Carlisle becomes managing editor he stops any story about Hayes. He is trying to bury the whole family, I think. One week, almost every paper has mention of someone in the family. The next week, as far as he's concerned, they don't exist. And it isn't just him. This is when Stone comes into the picture. Stone takes over the corner office upstairs that same week."

"When I saw you rummaging in that pile, I guess you just shook a piece of the past out of me."

Frank's heart tightened. He had always felt in touch with the city where he had grown up. Now, hearing this from Carl, he realized that he knew nothing of its past. For a man that was under the assumption that he knew his work fully, and the city was his work, it was more than a blow. Carl sensed Frank's feeling.

"Don't worry about it, Frank," said Carl. "Things that are in the dark for a long time often stay that way. It was a strange happening in a distant past."

"What do you mean?" asked Frank.

Carl had to think for a moment. "I think that maybe Carlisle got burned by Hayes."

"Come on, Carl. What do you mean burned? We've all been burned by somebody. It didn't hurt his career. How could it? His family owned the bloody paper at the time. What the hell does he care?"

"I'm not sure, Frank. I think it was about more than just the stories that were written. Carlisle was from the same group. They both had money and they both went to the same schools and belonged to the same clubs. I guess they were boyhood friends at one point. They all knew each other back then, Carlisle, Stone and Hayes. I think Carlisle probably thought that Hayes had done enough to the little community, he'd raked them over the coals, had gotten them caught up in a drama that was being played around him as the central character. Maybe Carlisle decided to stop giving Hayes any attention because he didn't deserve it. It seemed that Carlisle was happy to never have to write about Hayes again or hear his name. He was glad Hayes was gone."

Again, both men sat in silence.

"Frank?" came a man's voice. It startled them and they looked up. It was Councilman Kawaja.

"Councillor," said Frank almost with a sneer, instinctively returning to his cocky, cynical journalist self. "You know Carl Stanley, my editor."

"Councillor," Carl said in the same tone, same inflection.

"Frank, I didn't know this was going to be a panel discussion."

"Just leaving," said Carl. He left without saying goodbye. The councillor sat down and began speaking without Frank prompting him. Frank took out his notepad and began to write.

Chapter 5

When a good story hits a reporter, there's usually a buzz of some sort. It's like winning a lottery. It can mean so many things. Careers have been made on one story. Fortunes have been made. The rights for books and movies sold. Robert Redford or Al Pacino might even play you in the film adaptation. These were stories that reporters would fight over. They would pray to get them or stumble upon them.

Why hadn't someone dug this Hayes thing up? Frank couldn't believe what Carl had said. What the hell was all that bullshit? Carl was too hard to accept some fucked-up tradition to not print any stories about Hayes. That was crap. Frank had seen Carl tell Carlisle to fuck off right in the editorial room. Carl had stood in front of him, daring him to say something. The publisher staring up at his city editor, his lip quivering in front of the news staff. Carl just stood there, almost indifferent.

And what about the way Carl told Frank about Hayes? It was all too calculated. If Carl wanted Frank to not write about Hayes, he would have just told him. Carl would have said in passing, "Frank, none of that Hayes shit hits my desk." It would have been that easy. Instead, Carl went out of his way to make Frank interested.

Frank thought for a moment.

"Christ almighty," he said to himself. He reconfigured his thinking.

The next day Frank went to the office even though it was his day off. He walked into the editorial room and headed to his desk. He looked through his mail and turned on his computer. He heard the whirr of the fan. It seemed comforting somehow. He put his hand on the top of the hard curved plastic back of the machine. As the electricity ran into its circuitry, booting up its operating system, heating up its insides, Frank couldn't help but feel the thing was alive. It was remarkable. This man-made beast was awe-inspiring. With the flip of a switch and a few wire connections, Frank could contact any part of the world. He could experience – at least virtually – anything the world offered, and then make it home for dinner.

The screen burst with colour and the "Welcome to Macintosh" splash screen. He thought about the manic personalities behind the invention of his computer. They didn't rest, that group. What they gave you was the idea of personal power.

Frank often looked at the computers, televisions, radios, photocopiers, and tape recorders all around the office. He considered all the power that must be plugged into the building. He thought about those huge power line towers that he saw up north the previous weekend. It was truly remarkable.

He went over to the other office machine he loved, the coffeemaker, and poured himself the last of the pot. It smelled strong and must have been sitting for some time. Frank placed the pot onto the hot plate and put more coffee into the filter. He pushed a red button on its side and the machine filled with water. It sounded like a tap running. Then, in a little under thirty seconds, delicious coffee came running down into the pot.

He took his coffee back to his desk, sat down, and sorted

through the mail. Letters from concerned citizens, no doubt, all saying what a crackpot he was. Frank chuckled to himself. He was doing a bad job. Not only did the entire office know it, now readers also knew. He threw them back on his desk. The light on his phone was flashing. Frank dialed his extension. After his message ended, Frank typed in his access code. The female voice of the phone system told him he had three new messages. Frank laughed at the way these systems walked you through the whole drill. The female voice said, "Here is your first new message."

"Frank, this is Stan Kawaja. I can't believe how incorrect you got everything yesterday. Please call me about that. I'd like the chance to clear those mistakes up." He deleted it.

"Hi Frank, it's Willie, just called to say hi. Call me if you get a chance, but I know you won't and even if you did I won't be able to answer the phone anyway because I'll be running around all day again so...just...hi. See ya."

Frank saved Willie's message. If things got tough later he'd listen to it again. The sound of her voice was very soothing.

"Frank, this is John Carlisle. I was wondering if you could come up and see me when you get in. No need to call, just come straight up." Frank did not move. He had spoken to John Carlisle only a few times since he joined the paper. He had been introduced to him when he was hired and they spoke briefly every year at the Christmas party, when Carlisle made a point of saying hello to all the staff before he and his wife ducked out to their home in the country. This was John Franklin Carlisle, publisher and former majority owner of one of the largest daily newspapers in the country. He couldn't move. The message had stopped running and he had been forwarded to an operator. "Newsroom. Can I help you? Hello...hello..." the receptionist said.

Frank came out of his paralysis.

"Oh... Sorry, it's Frank Medved, I just...never mind. Sorry." Frank hung up. He didn't know what to do. He wasn't even supposed to be there. It was his day off after all. Could he slip out and pretend he hadn't been there? No, too many people had seen him. Ducking out would only make things worse. Frank looked around the room for Carl, but he didn't see him. Frank picked up the phone and pressed zero. The receptionist came back on the line.

"Newsroom."

"Hi, it's Frank Medved again. Is Carl here?"

"Oh, hi Frank," she said. Frank could never remember her name. "No. Sorry, Frank. He isn't in yet."

He thought for a second. How bad could it be, really? Maybe Carlisle just wanted to explain why he had sent that message down with Carl. Frank had been at the paper for four years without incident. What was he worried about? Carlisle must know that Frank was just made a columnist. He was young for a columnist. It was an achievement. Carlisle was a shrewd guy. He must know.

"Frank," said the receptionist, still on the line, "can I do anything else for you?"

"Yeah, could you transfer me to Carlisle's office."

"Sure." There was a click and then ringing. Frank would see if he was in. The message said to just go on up but Frank knew better than to act that casually with people like Carlisle. When they said "just come on up," they meant call and make an appointment. Frank also knew that that, in itself, was a privilege.

"Mr. Carlisle's office," said one of his secretaries. Carlisle had two.

"Yes, this is Frank Medved in Editorial. Mr. Carlisle left a message that I, uh, for me to come and meet with him. Is he in by any chance?"

"Just a moment." There was a click and the occasional beep letting you know that you were on hold.

"Mr. Carlisle can see you now," she said.

"Ok...I'll be up, um, right away." He stood up. He looked over at the back of the editorial room and saw the steps that led up to the executive offices. He reached up and touched his neck. He didn't have a tie on. He was wearing a jacket and luckily he had his dressier pants on. He had also shaved that morning. He looked around to see if he could borrow a tie from anyone on the floor. He could go over to the business department. How would that look, though? No, he forgot about the tie business and wondered if he should try to sneak up the stairs. That wouldn't work either. How the hell could he get across the room and up the stairs without someone noticing? And if they noticed him trying to make it so no one noticed then they would really talk.

"Fuck it," he thought. He walked over to the staircase and took the stairs two at a time. He remembered what a career counsellor had once said: When you go into the interview, find your place of power. Find that event that makes you think you're a king. The day you felt better than any other day and then try and visualize it.

Frank got to the top of the very long staircase, went through the large glass doors, and walked up to the receptionist's desk.

"Hello," she said cheerfully.

"Hi, Frank Medved to see Mr. Carlisle." She picked up the phone and pressed a button.

"Frank Medved? Okay." She put the phone down and looked up at him. "Just a minute."

"Thanks," he said. Before he could look up a woman was standing beside him.

"Mr. Medved, come this way please." He followed obediently. They walked down a hallway with walls made of a dark wood. He figured it was mahogany. The floors were covered with a plush carpet and it was very quiet. He looked into the open offices as they passed them. Each contained a white man in a dark suit, white shirts with French cuffs and large gold cuff links, looking over papers or reading something on a computer. It was strange.

Frank followed the woman through what seemed to be a half-mile of offices. They turned and stood in another reception area. A woman sat typing behind a desk. Another desk was empty. He figured this was his escort's.

"Wait here," she said. She knocked on a large, dark wooden door with *John Franklin Carlisle* engraved on a large brass plaque. She walked in. Frank thought about the power she must have. He should really write a piece on the power of the executive secretary. That story could shake the establishment to its knees.

The light in that area seemed to come from everywhere and nowhere. Frank didn't see any light fixtures and yet there was light. He heard the faint buzz of electric power. He assumed it came from the computer terminals on the desks of the secretaries. The other secretary, busily working, had an antique desk. There were no cube sectional desks in this part of the building. Because of this, all the wires that came into the computer terminal – the phone line and all the other devices – lay there in a tangled mess. There were no special spots for the cords and plugs like on his gray laminate and particleboard desk. The tangle went from the desk to the floor and off into a corner that Frank couldn't see. She was definitely plugged in. She had enough wires to start her own radio station.

The woman came out of the office and shut the door behind her.

"Just a minute," she said and sat down at her desk. She too had an old desk that wasn't built to accommodate the new technology of the modern workplace. Frank stood in the middle of the large open area, his hands in his pockets, wondering if he should just tell her that he's quitting and that she should just pass on that message. It was a serious option until there was a quiet tone and she picked up her receiver. She said yes and stood up, went to the door and opened it.

"You can go in now." She smiled. Frank thought that this could be the last face he ever saw, because he might never leave that room alive. The image made him laugh and he did so pretending to cough into his hand. He said thank you and walked in. When he got inside the office, he thought that he very well could be right.

The room was huge. There were tall windows from floor to ceiling. The furniture was, if that were possible, of a darker and redder wood than that of the hallway. It made the room, even with the light coming from the windows, dark and a little sinister. Standing by the large desk at the far end of the room was Carlisle. He waved Frank in. Sitting beside him, writing in a notepad, was another man. His face wasn't noticeable at first. He was immersed in whatever he was writing. He had grey hair and seemed to be Carlisle's contemporary. *Holy shit.* Frank's stomach dropped. His hands went cold and clammy. He had trouble walking and stopped halfway to the desk.

It was Stone. What the fuck was going on? Carlisle smiled and told him to take a seat. Frank moved in and tried to speak, but all he managed was a nod. His eyes moved back to the man at the desk, who did not even acknowledge his presence

"Well, Frank," began Carlisle with what was obviously a forced smile, "how are things as a columnist?" Frank looked up from Stone to Carlisle. He shifted in his chair. He crossed his legs.

"Shaky to begin with, but I expect them to get better." He knew there was no point in lying, although that was his inclination.

"Don't worry, things don't always have great beginnings. It is how they end that matters," said Carlisle. It seemed as if he were giving Frank his credo. Stone did not take his attention from his writing. Carlisle stood by the desk, not moving.

"Can I get you anything? Coffee, perhaps a mineral water?" Frank was dying for a coffee but shook his head no.

"Frank." Carlisle said dramatically. Here it comes, thought Frank. Find that moment. That moment when you felt better than you ever have before. All he could think of was Willie naked. He shook his head to rid himself of that image, it was too distracting. "Carl came to see me yesterday. You know that, don't you?"

Frank nodded. Stone continued to write, oblivious to the conversation and perhaps even to the other two men in the office.

"Well, um, good, I'm glad that he was honest with you." Carlisle didn't seem happy about that. His feeling about Carl's talk the day before had been correct. Thank God for Carl. "You know, Frank," Carlisle put his hands behind his back and looked up as if searching for inspiration, "every paper has a way of categorizing the news and, well, are you a student of history?"

Frank looked at him blankly. What the hell kind of a question was that?

"Yes, sir. I mean, I studied history at university."

"Which university was that?" asked Carlisle. Frank couldn't take his eyes off of Stone, writing at the desk.

"Toronto, um, the University of Toronto," he said.

"Good school, first rate," said Carlisle. Frank heard the same slight British accent that Trish's friend Richard had. He leaned back in his chair and his attention was drawn to a painting hanging on the wall. It was a large thing, a landscape of some battle. There were soldiers in blue and red in clumps throughout. In the foreground was a man dressed in blue on a white horse. He did not wear a hat like the men who stood beside him. Frank guessed that he was the leader.

"Yes," Frank finally said.

"Well, yes, history is indeed a great thing. It can teach us a great deal if we allow it. Each situation that modern man can experience has already been lived at some point in history. And that fact allows us to learn so that we can not only avoid situations that may arise, but we can also look to great leaders of the past and witness how they themselves dealt with problems." Carlisle stopped to ponder the great thing he felt he had just said. Frank studied the man in front of him, writing, unmoved.

Carlisle continued, "The great men of history are many things but they have something particular. It is strength. Look at them and their actions and find one common thread. Strength." Carlisle had turned to face the window, and Frank suspected that if he walked out, it would be a long while before either Carlisle or Stone would realize he was gone. In fact, it would probably take the secretary outside coming in to tell them.

"Strength can indeed play itself out in many ways," said Carlisle. "One that I prize is the strength to learn from those great men and put into practice the things that they have done. To this end, I study their actions. If they are military men, I study their battles, learn their sacrifices, avoid their failings. I feel, and have said so on many occasions, that it is incumbent upon all of us to learn from history. Do you agree so far?"

"Yes," Frank almost spat out at him. He was in a state of shock.

"Good, good," said Carlisle. "Because of what I have said, we can then conclude that history is a living thing. It is like a great wise man, sitting beneath a tree somewhere, by a river, waiting to give enlightenment. But, like all wise men, it gives us wisdom in riddles. It is up to us to solve those riddles. If we are unwavering in our principles and our morality then those things that we attain can open a world to us that is beautiful and rewarding. But if the riddles are solved without the necessary virtue, their answers may never truly be revealed to us, and then we are unhappily faced with the misfortune of reliving the pain of all those who have gone before us. Do you think I am correct in this assertion?"

"Oh, very much so," said Frank. He knew that was a loaded question. He just wasn't sure why he was being asked it. He knew that Carlisle felt superior to almost anyone he'd ever met. Perhaps he was trying to prove that point. But really, he had no idea what the hell Carlisle was talking about. In fact, the whole event was so surreal that he only wanted it to run its course without causing too much commotion.

"Good then," said Carlisle. Frank forced himself to take his eyes from Stone and look at Carlisle. Carlisle was also staring at Stone. His writing continued. Carlisle coughed awkwardly. Stone stopped for a moment as though he had lost a thought and then began again. He completed the line, ended with a period that seemed like a thunder clap and then finished with an elaborate stroke that Frank assumed was his signature. With that, he put his pen down. He looked up at Carlisle. It was a short glance but it made Carlisle take a step back. Stone looked over to Frank. Frank looked at his eyes. They were steel grey and cold. Frank felt a shiver.

"Frank, let me make myself very clear," Stone began. "I have little time for fussing with the minutia of the many concerns that fall within my influence. At times, though, no matter how I might try to deflect these details," Stone looked up at Carlisle, "I find it necessary to make decisions for those people I have put in my stead." He left his gaze on Carlisle. Frank could see some of the air being squeezed out of the man's body. He turned back to Frank.

"Frank, may I be blunt?" he said, standing up from the desk and walking toward a window at the side of the office. He was a tiny man. This startled Frank and his jaw dropped open slightly. He quickly regained his composure, cleared his voice, and replied, "Of course."

"Thank you," Stone said, going too far, in Frank's mind, to be polite. Stone could say whatever he wished to Frank. He didn't need to ask to be blunt. Nor did he have to thank Frank for the privilege. Everyone in the room knew that. "This country is in trouble, Frank. It is in trouble and it can only be helped by people like ourselves – intelligent, visionary people. My life has been cursed by the fact that I am able to see things clearly, without sentimentality, and without fear of sentimentality clouding my judgment or my actions." Stone turned to look at Frank. The glare from the window gave him a ghostly appearance.

"I see this in you as well, Frank, and that's why I suggested that you should become a columnist. I might add that you are the youngest columnist that I employ at any of my eighty daily or one hundred and twenty-three weekly information properties." Stone allowed that point to hang for a moment. Frank knew its significance. He hadn't been promoted because of the work he had done, not fully. As was so often the case with Stone, Frank was elevated by him personally because he shared the same ideas as Stone did. Frank thought about what that meant. He had always thought that he and Stone had vastly differing points of view. Perhaps they did, but Frank now realized that perhaps it didn't matter.

"I see in you, Frank, a new breed of Canadian journalist. Removed from the old ways of 'stay the course,' parochial ideas." Stone walked toward Frank. "You are unhindered by those things that make Canada a backward nation. One that I can't even live in because its inward-looking self will not allow its true strength to shine through. You know that too." He stood over Frank. "I have seen it in your writing and in your candour." Again, that point hung between the two men for a moment. Stone appeared almost child-sized before him. Although Frank was sitting, they almost viewed each other eye to eye.

"For some reason, this has changed recently. That worries me." Stone turned, walked back to the desk, and sat down again. Carlisle shuffled over as Stone did this.

"I need you to remain the writer and thinker you are. Not some new found nostalgist. I need you to have the strength of your convictions and to understand your duty." Stone said with passion in his eyes. His show of emotion made Frank uncomfortable. After a silence, Stone continued coldly.

"I hope that this bit of advice has been taken to heart. Good day." With that, Stone took up his pen again and began to write one more.

"Thank you," said Carlisle, speaking up from his position. Frank looked at Stone writing away and stood up.

"Thank you," he stuttered to Carlisle. He turned and walked to the door, opened it and left. Outside, the secretaries behind their desks did not notice. He followed the path back down the hall toward the staircase, down to the editorial floor. He made no noise as he walked.

He stopped at the staircase. He thought about the meeting he had just had. He did not know what it meant. From the bottom of the stairs he could hear the voices of reporters on the phone and the tapping of fingers on keyboards. He walked toward it.

"Oh Frank, you're kidding," said Cash, grabbing a clump of his hair. His eyes and his mouth wide open, he was thinking of what to say next. Cashman Gillis was an old war horse of the reporting world. He had started his career in radio in the early 1960s and had stayed in it all his life. Even when it became fashionable to get into TV, Cashman, a handsome enough man, if a little ragged, stayed with his first love. After years of toiling for little money and even less recognition, he was enjoying his time as a professor of Journalism at Ryerson University. Frank and Cash had become friends after speaking at a Forum on Minorities in the newsroom. Representing their respective media instruments, they were soundly beaten down by the very vocal and militant minority leaders in the crowd. Afterwards, they went to a bar and got drunk. They'd been friends ever since.

"I mean, Christ. Stone was right there? Oh fuck, I might have belted him in the teeth if I was in your shoes." Cash laughed and then took a long drink from his gin and tonic. "Just think Frank, you're one of Stone's boys."

"Well, I didn't think that was an option," said Frank. He too took a long drink. The cold lager against his throat felt good. He didn't relish the fact that he was one of Stone's boys.

Those who didn't like Stone or his ways referred to his charges, the hand-picked people who ran his newspapers and wrote his opinion columns, as Stone's boys. They were usually younger versions of Stone. Many were brash, most weren't that bright. What they did have in common was that they either intuitively knew what Stone wanted written, or seemed to be on his wavelength. Frank had always considered them mere yes-men, nothing more. Now, suddenly, he was one of them.

Frank had called Gillis to talk about what had happened that morning. They met at his favourite pub, which was just off of Yonge Street near Wellesley. Gillis liked it because it was friendly, small, and you could have a decent conversation without raising your voice. He also liked it because it was far enough away from the school so that no students frequented it, yet close enough to pop in for a drink between classes. Cash's drinking problem was one of his greatest assets and greatest weaknesses. It had robbed him of years, cost him his marriage, and in some part, stalled his career. And yet, he was great to have a drink or two with, and often that was all he would have. But you wanted to get away from him if he was about to go on a binge. Frank had stayed up with Cash many nights – suicide watch was what he thought of it.

"Tell me again," said Gillis. "You walk in and there is Stone, sitting there scribbling away. What a son of a bitch. He did the same thing to me." This memory made him laugh. He grabbed a tuft of hair with one hand and his drink with the other. He had interviewed Stone years before. That was why Frank had called him. It was back when he had just begun to get involved with the world of newspapers. Stone had decided that the mining industry was not glamorous enough. That was what Gillis said in his article. Stone's family had been involved in mining and other natural resources industries. Stone's father, Harold Sr., was reputed to be a man of great courage and temper, and had personally helped to begin the thriving mining industry in Canada.

"The son of a bitch figures he's some sort of royalty because he's always having those parties," said Gillis, referring to the lavish functions Stone was known to host. He ordered two more drinks. Frank knew he had to start asking for specific information, as he'd be drunk soon.

While Frank was anxious to tell Willie about what had happened, he knew that it was going to be a busy day for her. He could wait to talk with her about it. At this point, though, he had to get what he could out of Gillis before he started telling too many old stories.

"Tell me about the man, Cash. What the hell was that all about?" Cash leaned forward and a serious look came over his face. Sensing that Frank was a little rattled, he decided to put the jokes aside.

"You see Frank, from what I know of Stone, he's a pompous son of a bitch, but he's shrewd. He summoned you for a reason that you may or may not know about. You say that the column wasn't going well, so that isn't a big deal." Gillis was making no attempt to tell Frank that wasn't the truth so he had to believe that things weren't going well. "So, why are Carlisle and Stone sitting there? And why the theatrics? Well, maybe they were feeling you out. Stone is like every other man in his position, he's standing very tall on our shoulders, only the short bastard thinks the reason he has a clear view is because we're down on our knees in front of him." The drinks arrived and Gillis took one. "It's common enough and you see it everywhere. But the little bastard doesn't want anyone shouting out that he's naked as he's prancing around – sorry for mixing metaphors – and he especially doesn't want anyone who matters shouting it. Suddenly, for some reason, you seem to matter. And I bet something is making him think that you can see that little prick of his dangling away, in plain view." Gillis sat back with one hand on his head and his drink in the other. He thought about what he had just said and looked as though he found it fascinating. He took a drink.

Frank thought about it. Cash was right. Stone hated to be challenged and went out of his way, with what seemed like an obsession, to rebuke and refute anything that showed him or his actions in a negative way. What about Carl? He had run up to see Carlisle after he saw him searching for information about Hayes. At least that was what he said. Maybe he had gone up to see Stone.

"Cash, tell me about the time you interviewed Stone."

Cashman Gillis sat back, rubbed his head, and pulled on his beard. He was from Cape Breton and like most of the natives of that part of Canada, had a contemplative side that was infused into his daily life. Frank had always thought it strange that such philosophical people could also be so emotional. Probably because Frank had learned his ideas on life from his time in university. It was strange how grand notions could be reduced to such boring pronouncements of faith. Cash Gillis didn't know how to be boring. Neither did his brethren. Because of it, Frank thought him fascinating and completely without pretense. More then a little bit of a contrast from the man of whom he was about to speak.

"Well, Frank, it is important for me to tell you first that as far he's concerned, the interview never happened. He denies it to this day."

"How does he manage to deny something that happened?" asked Frank. "He of all people, the grand litigator of the press, should realize that the lack of a lawsuit would make it almost a fact in the eyes of every reporter who has ever heard of him."

"It all stems from how the meeting happened. He heard that I was," Gillis finished his gin and waved at the waitress, "doing an hour documentary on the new leaders of the decade. This was in the early eighties. Anyway, he wanted to be on that list. I can only guess. His press man – think about that – he had a full-time press agent, for himself, not for his company. His press agent, who was an old CP reporter I had worked with at Queen's Park, convinced me that Stone was at least worth speaking to. I decided to fly to London to interview him. The CBC was paying, so I figured that the trip was worth it, and I would at least get a chance to see some friends from across the pond.

"We met at his building. A small thing with a few people running around, not doing much. He wasn't quite the press baron he is today. Stone took me into his office and talked at length about things like the Cold War, Kennedy and Nixon. He loved Nixon. He tried to tell me how Reagan was the answer to the world's prayers. He told me about meeting Reagan.

"We went from his office to a place where he usually had dinner. He continued talking, and, of course, I let him talk. Why ask questions of someone who wants to tell you everything? He spoke to me about what he had achieved from his modest beginnings and that his place in Canadian history was not yet written. Well, the more pompous he became, the more I drank. And when I had a little too much to drink, well, that's when I finally started asking questions.

"How much money did your father leave you?' That was my first question, I think. He gave me a long dirty look. He told me that it wasn't relevant. 'Don't you think that being thirty-five and being a multimillionaire on money just given to you means that your beginnings were more than modest?' He didn't even look at me. The one that really got him mad was, 'Why didn't you run off and join the army like your brother did during the Second World War? Wasn't your brother actually a year younger than you? He was only sixteen when he managed to lie his way into the army. You were eighteen in January of 1945 and you didn't join. How did it feel when you heard that your younger brother had died fighting for your freedom to turn the millions your father left you into even more millions?'" Gillis laughed and grabbed the tuft of hair that was now sticking up on the top of his head. "Holy fuck, he was mad as hell. But at least I got the bastard to stop ruffling his feathers." Gillis laughed again. The waitress came with the third round of drinks. Frank knew that he had to finish talking to Gillis before the fourth round.

"Well, what happened then? After you told him about his brother dying. Is that a true story?" asked Frank.

Gillis nodded. "Yeah, I had done the research before the interview. I spoke to an old friend and business partner of his. He told me everything. He didn't like Stone much."

"I would think that when the boy's parents found out, they would've got Stone's brother the hell out of there," said Frank.

"Not that group. They were probably prouder than Mary and Joseph. Anal retentive loyalists with their empire and their monarchy and 'there will always be an England,' ahgg." Gillis broke off. His parents were Irish Catholic, straight from the old country.

"What happened about him denying the interview?"

"He was very angry." Gillis sounded as though he was surprised Stone had reacted that way. "He looked at me for a while and didn't say anything. I asked him what he thought a true measure of success should be for his generation. Should they be judged differently, having benefitted so much from the post-Second World War world without suffering to achieve it? He was fuming then. He almost couldn't contain himself. He got up and went to the bathroom for almost a half hour. That's how I got proof that the interview happened. While he was sulking somewhere, I asked the waiter for the cheque. He didn't want to bring it because Stone always paid. But I insisted, the CBC was picking up the tab, and since Stone was gone so long, he brought it. I had the credit card slip to prove that I was there. I even got the waiter to put down my name and Stone's and sign the back." Gillis let Frank ponder what he had said. Then, he continued.

"You see, I got him. I let him know that some people didn't believe his crap. I let him know that just because you tell a lie long enough, it doesn't become the truth. And I'll tell you that men like Stone don't like the truth being thrown in their face. It goes against all the things they've taught themselves to believe. Their rationalizations, you see, young Frank." Gillis was drunk now. His glory years were gone, except for the drinking and the ranting. "They sit down and screw every person they can until they achieve what they want. These are passionless people, men mostly, who don't even sleep with their wives because it may affect their rest. For them, all that matters is the conquest. The conquest is everything. The rest is just kids' stuff. The act of living for them is simply an annoyance between business meetings. And in the end, they are happy for it. That is the true shame. They live wonderfully fulfilled lives, these men, and they do not think that their lives are anything less than that. They cherish every moment of banal, shallow pleasure. They die happy, this group, they die old and happy and without remorse, always thinking that theirs was the true and righteous path. That's what the dogmatic life will get you. The ability to screw others without regret, no matter how much those people may be your betters, and do it in the name of family or religion or the right thing. All of that without questioning what the right thing might actually be. Do you understand, Frank? I think you do. Your people understand the value of humanity and suffering. These people do not. The worst part is that they can't stand people like you, Frank, because your humanity makes you question their dogma." Gillis fell silent. He grabbed his tuft of hair again as though he was searching his brain. Frank could almost see the electric impulses flashing through Gillis's skin. All the nerves running through the brain, like electric wire into the world's most complex mainframe, the human brain. Gillis looked up. He took his drink and finished it. He started again.

"Do you know what they hate worse, Frank? It's when one of their own shows them that their lives are pointless. A traitor is not only to be hated, but also feared. Stone's brother was a boy of great passion and conviction. He upstaged Stone when he died in that bloody war. Stone hated him for that. Then there was that Hayes fellow." Frank nearly missed the name. Gillis had often gone on with his lectures. Frank listened quietly without really paying attention, or he would find reason to leave. Sometimes he would not remember a thing Gillis had said.

"Hold on." Frank nearly had to shout to stop him. "Did you say Hayes?"

"Oh yes, Hayes. He was in Stone's class at that school that type goes to. Sorry, Frank. You went to one of those too, didn't you? A cheaper Catholic copy, but still it was one of those, wasn't it." Frank allowed the comment to go. He wanted to hear more about Hayes.

"What do you know about Hayes?"

"Well, not much. It was when I was doing my research. Apparently Hayes and Stone were rivals at school. They didn't like each other much. Well, Stone didn't like Hayes much. That was for sure."

"How do you know?"

"I asked Stone's first wife. She's passed away now, but at the time she was willing to talk about him. Her love for him was all gone."

"I thought Stone had only married once."

"That is the party line. A lot of these CEO types rid themselves of their first wives because they can't stand having anyone around who knew them before they got their power and money. They want some pretty young thing who will do as they say, when they say, and look good doing it." Gillis was spitting with anger now.

"Stone's first love told me about his early life. That isn't well documented anywhere. She told me about his brother and about this fellow Hayes. Apparently – and this is what he had told her so we can only imagine how it really went – Stone organized a major black tie event in aid of the war effort. This was back when they were at school together. Do you believe that? Stone's younger brother was off fighting in the war while

91

he was raising funds at home. Anyway, Hayes, who was no lover of the war, is asked to be a speaker at this thing, by virtue of a vote. There are other speakers as well. Some may have been federal politicians. That must have made Stone really red. Here he is working hard to organize this thing, there is a vote for a speaker, and he isn't chosen. With an ego like his, no wonder he has nothing good to say about the place now.

"So, Hayes is to speak. At this time, near the end of the war, there are a lot of reports coming out of Poland and other places about what has been happening to the Jews. They are unsubstantiated, but they are coming out little by little. Most people either don't believe it or don't care at this point.

"Hayes shows up to the dinner with a young Jewish boy who doesn't speak a word of English. He's just gotten out of Europe somehow and he and his mother made it to Canada. God knows how the hell Hayes finds this kid to bring him along but that is beside the point. It turns out that his father had been sent to one of those camps, and, well, they never heard from him again. The boy stays in the kitchen until Hayes is to speak." Gillis took a drink.

"Hayes and Stone sit at the same table together with all the other people who are going to speak. Stone, being the organizer, isn't going to miss his chance to sit with some MP or other who has decided to attend and give a speech. Hayes is first. He talks for a while about the war and the suffering it has caused for those at home and in Europe, and then he brings out this boy. Now when I say boy, apparently he wasn't much younger than Stone and Hayes. As the boy stands beside Hayes, probably not quite sure what is going on, Hayes tells the room about what the boy has been through and how the fact that he is still alive is, in many respects, a miracle. He goes on to say that, like most Jews, his life meant nothing to the Nazis. Jews are killed without warning. He talks about the fear and about the death camps.

"Strong stuff. Apparently Hayes has the place near silence. Then his speech turns. He begins to praise the people who are laying down their lives for the safety of not only those people in North America or Europe, but also the world. He talks about the fact that they have to make sure that such horrible events could never happen again. He tells them that they are the leaders of the future and that after the war it is up to them to rethink the way that men interact with each other and with the world around them. He talks about the need for decency, not only for all men but for all things, including nature and the animals. He tells them about the need for a better understanding of how nature works and the fact that Canada has become a great nation because of its resources. He tells them that it's up to them to take the victory that the courage of those young men in the war will give them and make a better future for the entire world. When he's done, he takes the Jewish boy's hand and raises it over his head. He tells them that every man would be the victor if they only have the courage to lead.

"Well, the place bursts into a roar that is thundering. The boys, the masters, and the politicians all begin chanting Hayes' name. It lasts almost a half an hour. The boys are acting as though it's a football game. They will beat their adversary on that day and then they will build a new world... It was glorious. Even the poor young Jewish boy, standing there, not really sure what was going on, began to clap. Hayes was smiling broadly. He was caught up in it, you see Frank. He thought he had accomplished something, had gotten through to them. For a brief moment, his whole world must have made sense. There were shouts and songs, and it took the Master of Ceremonies a long time to finally quiet the place down.

"But, here is the interesting part. Hayes returns to his seat and on the way, picks up a chair that was against the wall. He brings the boy with him, puts the extra chair beside his, and has the boy sit down.

"Now, Frank, you're too young to remember the days when Jews were treated badly. I can remember it though. I'm being obvious when I say that there wasn't a great deal of mixing going on. Of course, that was when people from Eastern Europe were considered to be of another race. Before a whole new group of dark-skinned people started immigrating here and becoming..."

"Cash," Frank stopped him before he entered one of his rants. Gillis looked at the table for a moment, rearranging some old demons. Cash smiled and continued, "The rest of the table nearly falls out of their chairs onto their big white Anglo-Saxon arses. The hush in the room is almost as loud as the applause that shook it a few moments before. Stone is turning red. The politicians won't even look at the boy. Hayes looks around and sees the reaction and is as stunned as they are. He can't believe it. Finally Stone stands up and goes over to Hayes and whispers, 'See here Hayes, what are you trying to prove? You're being unfair to everyone by having this boy sit here.'

"Hayes stands up and looks around the table. There are two MPs, the Dean of the College, a couple of bigwig alumni. I think even the Lieutenant Governor is there. He stands in front of that group and stares them down for a minute. He must have been confused and probably burning up inside. But he composes himself and after a tense few seconds says very coolly, 'If we are going to be truly victorious in this war then the victory must begin here.' And with that, he lifts up the table and turns it over, right onto all those bastards. The place erupts with shock and laughter. Hayes goes to the next table and knocks that one over. He goes to the next. Stone is screaming at him and the politicians are running for cover. Hayes gets about half a dozen tables flipped over before a couple of large football players drag him out. Absolutely incredible." There was a silence as Gillis thought about what he had just described. It was as though he himself had heard it for the first time.

"According to Stone's first wife, that was the last time that Stone and Hayes ever spoke. He fucking ruined Stone's big night. Of course that's all that little bastard got out of the whole thing, 'Hayes ruined my night to shine,' as though that were the sole purpose of the event and the reason Hayes made his point." Gillis thought for a moment. "Although," he said, his eyes glinting with a smile, "that'd be enough reason for me." He laughed and threw back his head in a wild, uncontrolled way that made him seem spastic.

When Gillis stopped his manic laughing, something caught his eye and he looked over Frank's head to the opposite side of the room.

"Frank, stick around. A couple of broadcast types are coming over. It could be a fun night." Gillis turned to watch them approach. The two girls were blond and thin. Dressed completely in black. Frank saw that Gillis was drunk.

"No, Cash. I should go," said Frank. Cash was not paying attention. Frank got up quickly, left enough money for his drinks and a couple of Gillis'. He slapped Gillis on the back and left before the girls arrived.

Magnetic North

Chapter 6

Frank heard Willie's keys in his front door. He grabbed a beer out of the fridge and an opened bottle of white wine. He took a large wine glass down from the cupboard. "Hey Willie," he called out, pouring wine into the glass. It was 7:30. He had been home for about three hours. Some Friday hours, he thought.

"Hi Frankie," she called back. He heard her slump into the couch. It must have been another hard day for her, he thought. It had been a tough week for both of them. As Frank entered the living room he saw Willie sitting on the couch. She had taken off her shoes and undone her suit jacket. It was one of those suits that only allowed for a bra to be worn underneath, and that was all Willie had on. Frank could see her black lace bra holding her breasts. Her stomach was lean and tanned. On days such as the ones he was having, he often thought of her body warm against his. It gave him the kind of comfort that could get him through anything. Frank never told her that, he wasn't sure how she would take it. Things had been going so badly at work that he thought about having sex with Willie all day until it got so distracting he had to leave the office.

"What are you looking at?" she said, a knowing smile on her face. She pulled her suit jacket open. One side fell off her shoulder and she allowed it to slip quickly from her arm. Frank put her drink down on the table and sat in the opposite chair. Willie took off her jacket and sat on the couch in only her bra and skirt.

"Tough day?" he asked her. She nodded as she took a long drink. Frank looked at her body.

"Hell of a day," she said, putting the glass down.

"You look tired," said Frank. He watched as she reached around her waist to loosen the zipper of her skirt. She shimmied it off and threw it on the floor. Frank took a long drink from his beer.

"I hope you're not going to just leave that thing there," he said. Willie didn't laugh.

"How was your day?" she asked him. He smiled at her. "Just fine." he said. He hadn't told her about his meeting with Stone and Carlisle. He wasn't sure why. Perhaps it was his embarrassment, his realization of his place in Stone's world.

"Good, then you can give me a backrub."

While Willie was dozing beside him, Frank found himself thinking, perhaps for the first time, about what he had been doing for the past four years. The stories, the interviews, and the judgments passed. They came so quickly to him. He was absolutely right every time and he knew it. When he looked at the problems that created the news that he reported, it all seemed so simple. He could have given them the right answers to solve the problems, only no one ever asked him. It wasn't his job to get involved. That never sat well with him all those years. There was always something that bothered him. He thought about those stories. How hollow all his insights seemed. How unfocused they were. They had no past and no future. Gillis had told him about a philosopher in Boston who had written a book that talked of the lack of perspective that most people in power had. The problem solvers of the world ran the machinery. They did it in a vacuum, plugging and replugging in numbers until the equation worked. His theory was that we live in a society without ideas. The ideas had been replaced by equations. And, somehow, the equations always worked out. That was fine, thought Frank, if the world ran on mathematical principles.

Frank lay on his side, caressing Willie's back, thinking about all these things. As he did, he couldn't help but think of Hayes. It was Hayes who had started all of this. Frank had never seen such scrambling over one word. He worked in a world filled with words, but none had ever caused this much stir before. None had ever made him fear for his job, and more importantly, rethink his job.

The phone rang. Frank reached to grab it before it woke Willie.

"Hello," he said quietly, to no avail. Willie stirred beside him.

"Is Willie there?" asked a woman with a familiar voice.

"Hold on," he said. He looked down at Willie. She didn't open her eyes but reached out toward Frank so he could place the phone in her hand. Frank gave the handset to her and she cleared the grogginess from her throat.

"Hello," she said, trying to sound awake. "Yes. Oh shit, yeah, yeah, I'm going, we're just getting ready..." Willie looked over at Frank and rolled her eyes. "Ok, ok. You're right, take it easy Maggie. I forgot, but we'll be there." Frank didn't like the implications of what Willie was saying. They were going out to some function that Willie had not only forgotten about but also forgot to tell him about.

Willie opened her eyes and looked at Frank. "No, no, we'll meet you there. Ok, sure, sure, ok, bye." Willie hung up.

Frank looked at her. "What?"

"Sorry Frank."

"What? What did you forget to tell me?"

"The Dress Down Ball is tonight."

"The what? The Dress Down Ball? What the fuck is the Dress Down Ball?" Frank said. He was trying not to sound unhappy. It was difficult.

Willie got up and went downstairs to the kitchen. Frank followed her. She let the tap run and then filled a glass with water. "Maggie is on the committee for the Dress Down Ball and..."

"Fucking debutantes. Another fucking fundraiser. Why don't I just have them direct deposit my whole fucking cheque into the various charities that your friends seem to be running. Better yet, why don't they just write a fucking cheque so we can stay at home." Willie came out of the kitchen and looked up at Frank, lips pressed together. She stopped him dead with one look.

"Frank, I forgot all about it and, to be honest, I don't want to go either, but don't start with that 'bad boy' street language you try and use. These are my friends." Frank steamed for a moment and then calmed down.

"No goddamn tuxedos," he said, trying to sound adamant.

"Now, Frank darling," she said "It's casual chic."

"Fucking casual chic," he began to laugh. "What the hell does that mean?"

"Jeans and pearls," said Willie.

"What the hell have I gotten myself into?" Frank asked.

"You watch yourself, Frank, or you might never get into it again," she turned and wiggled her ass at him for effect.

Willie and Frank got out of the cab at the corner of Queen and Yonge. They decided to walk the rest of the way to the Old City Hall building. It was a warm night and Willie was wearing a short black dress with thin spaghetti-like straps holding it onto her shoulders. Frank loved and hated the dress. She was incredibly sexy in it. He loved to see her in it but so did every other straight man. As much as he tried not to let it bother him, it was difficult. Willie knew it. She would send him looks when she wore it that made him melt and feel close to her. Frank had on his black jeans with a pair of black leather army-type boots. He had on a white t-shirt and a multicoloured vest that Willie picked out for him. The t-shirt was tight to his arms and he could feel his muscles move under it. It made him feel strong. He put his arm around Willie's thin shoulders. She leaned into his body and turned her face to kiss him.

Frank looked up and squinted at the night sky, trying to see the stars. A few bright ones were visible over the city's fluorescence, but not many. The walk was short and as they reached their destination they could see a crowd of people standing outside. It seemed that there was a line and Frank could hear some angry voices. A young woman stood on a chair and was speaking. It was Willie's friend Braunwyn. As Frank and Willie got closer, they could hear her yelling instructions.

"Did everyone hear me?" she said in a loud shrill voice. Frank couldn't tell if she was twenty-five or forty-five. Her hair, her make-up, the clothes that she wore were trendy and traditional at the same time. "Please stop pushing and everyone will get in."

"Hurry up, Brauny," said a tall hulk of a man standing near the back of the crowd. "We've got things to do, you know."

"Shut up, David," said Braunwyn. "We need to do this in an orderly manner." Braunwyn turned and saw Willie and Frank as they came up to the crowd.

"Finally, you're here. We've all been waiting!" Willie looked at Frank and then back at Braunwyn. She was surprised. "Come in. Quickly. Get things set up." She motioned them in and they obeyed without a word even though neither of them knew what she was talking about. Braunwyn got down from the chair, pulled them past the crowd, and through the doors. Frank saw two large men, one black and one white, standing inside. They had on tight t-shirts that showed every ripple of muscle on their large upper bodies. The shirts read, "Hired Goons Security Service." That's telling it like it is, thought Frank. As they passed the two bouncers, the doors closed behind them.

"Hi Braunwyn," said Willie, leaning to give her a kiss on the cheek.

"Hi Willie," said Braunwyn, kissing back. Her voice was as shrill as it was outside. "Sorry I had to rush you in like that but 'somebody' oversold tickets again this year and 'somebody' left it for me to handle again."

"Where is 'somebody'?" asked Willie.

"She's somewhere inside on her fourth gin and tonic by now," said Braunwyn. She turned and looked at Frank. "You must be Frank."

"Sorry, Braunwyn, this is Frank Medved. Frank, this is Braunwyn," Willie said.

"Hi," said Frank offering his hand.

"So, this is Frank," said Braunwyn, looking him over from top to bottom.

"Would you like me to turn around?" asked Frank.

"No need," said Braunwyn.

"He looks good, Willie, but he seems to be just a tad jumpy," said Braunwyn in a half-whisper.

"He drinks a little too much coffee." The girls laughed while Frank looked back toward the bouncers who were watching and sneering.

They walked up a long flight of stairs toward the sound of music and people talking. Frank started to feel the pounding beat of disco thumping in his chest. Braunwyn began to sway to the music as they climbed further, dancing in a very unprovocative way. White bread with mayo, thought Frank. Willie reached her hand into Frank's. At the top of the stairs they were met by a wall of bodies. A thick layer of smoke and the smell of cigars filled the air. Braunwyn disappeared through a hole in the crowd. Willie looked at Frank for a moment as they stood on the top step wondering how to navigate through the mass.

"We could always turn back and go home. We can always say we lost her," yelled Willie over the noise. She was clearly giving Frank the option to leave.

"No," said Frank leaning in to kiss her cheek. "We've come

all this way already." They smiled at each other and plunged into the sea of people.

The hellos and introductions began. Both Frank and Willie knew people at the ball. After Frank had gotten a beer for himself and a white wine for Willie, they both loosened up and began to enjoy themselves. Willie went to let Maggie know that they had arrived before she became too drunk to speak.

Frank stood against the wall and watched the laughing mob. Some were noticeably drunk already. Others were busy sizing up the action for the night. University all over again. Hostesses mingling with future husbands. It was a little different now, especially for the ones not yet married. Frats and dorm parties had been fun and the choices made for the sheer fun of it. Boys or girls they met or danced with or went home with, even dated, were fun or exciting or dangerous or brutal but they were all wrong. "She's so wrong for you, man," he would hear or say. "That Frank Medved is crazy, I mean really crazy," he was sure was said about him.

Now, though, the stakes were higher. The age of thirty approached. People were pairing off. Setting up house. Even playing Mom and Dad. For those still single, still unattached, the panic was setting in. Calls were being made to people who hadn't been spoken to in years. Old friends were getting another look. Blind dates were welcomed, even solicited. Frank wondered as he saw the mob circle the room, staggering a little more with each drink, a little louder, a little more boisterous, all the while moving with purpose and indent. Did they even know what cause they were supporting? Was it children with AIDS, or was it computer equipment for the deaf, or a new TV for a seniors' home? It didn't matter to them, he thought. Even he didn't know what the Dress Down Ball was in support of, nor at this point did he care.

Frank looked out over the heads of the crowd of people. Night after night, events like this were held. Night after night a new group of laughing drunkards searched the room, some wondering why they were there, others happy to be invited. Some hoped to see their photos in the little Toronto society columns. "Mr. and Mrs. Who-the-fuck-cares at the Brazilian Ball." Shit, the acknowledgment of a lifetime, thought Frank. That was until the wedding announcement was placed in *Town and Country* magazine. Or, better yet, they got to be on the committee and organize this year's event, finally, a fun event where everyone was going to have a great time and the place was going to be fabulously decorated and the food would be great and the dancing and the booze and the phone calls and the applause as the names of the committee members were announced. At that point, drunken stockbrokers would applaud as they gazed longingly at the woman to their right, trying to see down their low-cut gowns, praying their wives couldn't see them. He ran his hand over his head and headed back into the crowd.

Frank ran into one of the arts reporters from the paper, Jim Reynolds. He was there with his girlfriend, who worked as a VJ for MuchMusic.

They talked for a while, about the paper and about Frank's first weeks as a columnist. Even Jim knew things weren't great.

"Frank, you've just got to take it easy and it will all come out. Don't worry about it too fucking much." Jim wore a very sleek black three button suit; it looked hand-tailored. His hair was short on the sides and what remained, a thick blond shank, was pulled back and covered in gel.

"Dude, you've got to understand that you're in!"

Frank thought for a moment about what that meant. He was indeed "in." Stone had let him know that completely. He was also in danger of being pushed back out again. Maybe you shouldn't wish too hard for something, he thought.

A short, pudgy, sweaty-looking man walked up to the two of them. He looked familiar, but Frank couldn't place him.

"Hello James," said the greasy little fellow. Frank couldn't decide if he was a teenager, Frank's contemporary, or a man in his mid-fifties.

"Hello Ronald," said Jim. "You're still dressing like a fucking grandfather, aren't you."

"Looks continue to be your only way of discerning the good from the bad, isn't it James?" said Ronald.

"Once you've realized the whole bunch of us are fucked up, then the only distinguishing characteristic is how you dress. Your style. The whole point of the thing is to get laid and Ronny baby, I know you ain't getting any."

"I see that you are still dating Melissa," said Ronald. "I guess I lost the bet. I thought she would have been back with her own kind by now." Ronald began to laugh. Jim didn't. "Who's your friend, James?"

"Ronald Hacker, this is Frank Medved," said Jim. "Frank, this is Ronald Hacker. He's Melissa's cousin." Ronald Hacker. That's who he is, thought Frank. Ronald fucking Hacker. What the fuck was he doing at a party like this? What was he doing in Toronto?

Ronald held out his hand. Frank noticed how tiny and weak it was as they shook hands.

"Well, well. Frank Medved. This is an honour. One doesn't often meet a young lefty like you," said Ronald. "Probably because there are so few of your stripe left. No pun intended."

"Mr. Hacker," said Frank to the little man in front of him. "I've been reading your articles lately in the *Conservative Review*. You've truly been living up to the family name, haven't you." The little man's eyes fixed on Frank and narrowed. "Now, Ronald, don't look at me like that. This isn't the debating union you know. You've got to be able to back up stares like that in the real world." Frank took a drink from his beer bottle and chuckled to himself, feeling his chest puff up just slightly. Jim looked away. He wanted no part of the confrontation.

"I see that you've been promoted to the high position of spewing out the union position on current events for that rag that you work for. Shame it's not going well." Frank clenched his jaw. What a little shit, he thought to himself.

"Why is it, Ronald, that every one of your articles deals with how you don't want the government taxing you on all the income your parents gave you. You've become a bit of a one-trick pony don't you think?"

"I certainly hope you're not going to break into 'Solidarity Forever' Frank, it would be rather unbecoming to a social climber like you," Ronald said with a smile.

"Now fellas, that's enough," Jim said "We're here to have fun."

Frank ignored Jim. "How's the indictment going against your father, Ronald?" asked Frank. "Last time I checked, it didn't look good."

Ronald shot back quickly. "My father has given this country more than it deserves and now it is paying him back with this cheap stunt. I can't wait until he is cleared and he sues that French bastard up in Ottawa."

"He's not French, Hacker, he's Canadian and here's a newsflash: your father did it and they're going to take all his fucking money away and you'll be lost living in New York without a goddamn cent and then you'll come crawling home pushing some hard-working guy out of a job because Harold Stone will want you on his side." Frank felt his face flush.

"All right, boys." said Jim. "That's enough of that. Keep the politics to the fucking pages. We're here to have fun." Frank nodded to Jim and turned to look for Willie. Hacker looked at the floor for a moment.

"Well Frank," said Jim, "I see that you came here with Willie Rutherford. Are you two dating?"

"Yeah, yeah, well I think it's more than dating, really. Do you know her?" said Frank looking again at the crowd trying to spot Willie so they could leave.

"Well, sort of. My parents and hers were really close when they were younger. Just out of college. They had a falling out at some point, though."

"They can be hotheads," said Frank to Jim. "There are all sorts of events where one of them has lost his cool. I've heard a lot about an old uncle who ripped up that school that you went to."

"Oh, you mean Hayes," said Jim. Frank looked at him.

"Hayes?" said Hacker, looking up from the floor for the first time.

"Yes, that's right. Jim, what do you know about Hayes?" Frank ignored Hacker.

"Not much, really. He was a bit of a mythical figure around the school. He was a real shit-disturber and he got kicked out."

"Expelled, I believe they call it," added Hacker firmly.

"You went there too?" Frank asked Hacker.

"That's where I know James from," said the sweaty little man, trying to smile and seemingly trying to start again in a more friendly manner.

"I've heard a lot about Hayes recently," said Frank to Jim, hoping to get a response.

"You know who could tell you a lot about Hayes? Reginald Sloan." Hacker jumped in.

"Reginald Sloan?" said Frank. "I've heard that name before. He's an artist, isn't he?"

"That's an understatement," said Jim. "He's an industry. He has paintings in every gallery in the country."

"He also went to the College," said Hacker, beaming. He was associating himself with greatness.

Frank searched the crowd for Willie. Jim signalled to someone across the room and waved them over.

"Look Jim," said Frank, leaning toward him. "I've got to get the hell out of here. Can I call you tomorrow about Sloan?"

"Sure," said Jim, slapping Frank on the back. Frank turned to Hacker.

"Well Mr. Hacker, I'm sorry about earlier. It was nice to have met you, but nicer to be able to say goodbye." Frank turned and walked toward the bar.

Magnetic North

Chapter 7

The street on which Reginald Sloan lived was difficult for Frank to find. He drove around the neighbourhood for nearly an hour. Although the street map had indicated that it should be at the end of one street, it wasn't. Frank had to continue circling around because nearly every street in Cabbagetown was one-way. He was tired. He had only managed to get an hour and a half of sleep. He wasn't sure if it was the pounding beat that continued to thump in his ears long after he and Willie had left the party, or the idea of meeting Sloan that kept him awake. After they managed to say good night to what seemed like the hundreds of people Willie knew at the party, she told him that she thought that Sloan was a contemporary of Hayes and had gone to school with him.

Frank had called Jim Reynolds early on Saturday to get Sloan's phone number. Reynolds wasn't awake yet and wasn't happy to hear from Frank. In the end, he didn't have Sloan's number at all, and Frank had to look it up in the phone book. It wasn't hard to find. For some reason, Frank felt that Sloan wouldn't have a phone, would be unlisted, or the call would go to someone who screened his calls. He was sure that when the phone was answered, someone other than Sloan would be on the other end of the line. But in fact, when Sloan picked up, it was as though he was happy to talk to Frank. One of the benefits of being a reporter is that when you call someone you don't know early on a Saturday morning, they seem to understand; they assume that you must have a good reason. That was especially so of someone like Reginald Sloan, who had reporters calling him regularly.

Sloan was one of Canada's greatest living artists. Those were Willie's exact words. Although he wasn't well-known outside of Canada and Britain, he was the closest thing to a household name that an artist can be within Canada. His paintings sold for tens of thousands of dollars. Every major collection in Canada had a Sloan in it. Elementary school students heard his name spoken by their teachers. There were numerous articles about him and collections of his works were put in books that lay on the coffee tables of the cultured. Frank couldn't say he liked the work much. Willie had pulled a book out from a shelf when they reached her apartment. There was something murky about his work. Frank's narrow taste in art fell mostly on the painters of the turn of the century in France. He was drawn to great examinations of the human form rather than the abstracts that were Sloan's specialty. It hardly seemed to matter, though. Frank had not come to discuss his style. He only wanted to learn about Hayes. What he did find odd about Sloan's paintings was that they all seemed to be exclusively in shades of vibrant blue.

Frank came to the dead end street that he had passed twice before. On the map there was another street that ran off of it. From the top of the short, narrow drive, it didn't seem as though there was any road leading from it at all. Frank turned the car down the street and drove toward its end. As he swung around, he noticed a small dirt driveway. Frank drove into the alley and nosed the car forward. He saw three small houses tucked away amongst a thick growth of trees.

"Holy shit," murmured Frank in amazement. It was as

though he had walked into some small forest from a Brothers Grimm Fable. There were three cottages, surrounded by trees and flowers, on a dirt road in the middle of downtown Toronto. Incredible.

None of the houses had numbers on them. That must have been why Sloan had said the last house on the street rather than telling him the address. Frank walked past the first two houses. They were wooden structures, something you might see in a Nova Scotia town rather than the red brick usually associated with Toronto. All were painted in wild colours. One was light grey with pink and purple trim. The flowers in the garden in front were in full bloom and their fragrance hit Frank in the nose with a warm, moist scent. Frank found himself taking a long deep breath. The next house was white with red trim and black shingles. It also had a wonderfully landscaped garden filled with flowers and small trees. Frank thought it must be more in the Japanese style, but he realized after thinking it that he knew absolutely nothing about gardening. For some reason, seeing these displays made him wish he did.

The last house was Sloan's and it was drab by comparison. It was pale blue with a darker blue trim. The garden had been tended to, that was clear enough, but it wasn't lavish. There were two great pine trees that actually brushed up against the side of the house. The roof and eaves beginning to rot, likely because of the moisture from the trees and the fact that the sun seemed to never get to that part of the house.

Frank walked up the flagstone path to the door and knocked. He could hear a body stirring inside.

"Just a minute," came a call. Frank noticed through the frosted glazed window that the body went rushing upstairs. It seemed to not have any clothes on at all. Frank looked at his watch. It was 1:30 p.m. Frank saw a wooden fence that ran along the far side of the lane. If it wasn't for that fence and the lane he could swear he was on an island in the Atlantic or somewhere just off the coast. He closed his eyes and tried to breathe in the sea. The door opened behind him. Frank turned with a start. Standing in front of him was a man. His full head of grey hair had not been combed for days. He had not shaved recently, and his face was covered with grey stubble. His white shirt was covered in stains of blue. It was unbuttoned. A large covering of grey hair ran across his chest. The shorts he had on were worn out enough that Frank could tell that he was not wearing any underwear. The last bit of an unfiltered cigarette hung from his mouth.

"You must be Frank," said Sloan. His voice was deep and hoarse but gentle. There was a gravelly quality to it, most likely from the smoking.

"Yes," said Frank, "Frank Medved."

"Well, Frank Medved, come on in."

"Thanks." Frank walked into the house, stood just inside the door and allowed Sloan to close the door behind him.

"I thought we'd talk on the back patio. It sure is a nice day," Sloan said.

"That's fine," said Frank.

Sloan led Frank through the house and towards the back. Frank glanced into the living room as they passed. It had been turned into a studio and it looked like a disaster area. Obviously, Sloan painted with his canvases on the floor. There were no easels, but there were works-in-progress everywhere. Tones and tints of blue left their mark on everything. Patches of it covered the walls and floors. Some had managed to splatter onto the ceiling. Sloan was referred to as "Canada's Picasso"at one time because everything he did seemed to have a blue tinge to it. Blue blood, thought Frank.

They walked into the kitchen. There was a comfortable feel to it and Frank felt at home when they walked in. A basil plant in the window filled the room with its fantastic aroma. The sink, the fridge, and the table were old but spotless. Nothing like the studio. Sloan stopped. "Hold on a minute, would you?" he said. He reached into the sink and ran water over something in it. Frank looked at the walls of the kitchen. There were photos and articles pinned with thumb tacks. Frank took a closer look at some of the photos. One was Sloan with Andy Warhol.

"Wow, Andy Warhol," said Frank.

"Oh yeah. I met Andy when I lived in New York." He said, still rinsing away. There were photos of other famous people. Sloan receiving something from Governor-General Sauvé. Sloan wasn't smiling as he accepted whatever it was. Another photo showed him surrounded by a group of small Asian children. Beside it was an old, yellowed paper with handwritten verse on it.

> It may be likened to a worldly man.
> When he washes and bathes his body clean,
> Anointing it with good and fragrant oils,
> Adorning his head with a flowered headdress
> And clothing his body in white garments,
> He is called the son of a noble clan.
> It is even so with the homeless monk.
> For ever pure in conduct and virtue,
> Being clothed in garments of the Law,
> Perfect in deportment and appearance,
> He is called the true son of the Buddha.

There was a small, blurred inscription beneath the lines, perhaps the author's name. Another photo that Frank was particularly taken with showed Sloan in the pilot seat of a float plane.

"Do you fly?" asked Frank. Sloan was busy cleaning the small mess that his rinsing had left.

"Yes. I have my pilot's license. But, I haven't flown for years," he said, walking towards the end of the kitchen. "Let's go outside." He pulled the sliding door open and walked out onto the patio. Frank followed him. It truly was a patio, made from the same flagstone as the path in front. There were a few chairs, a table made of wrought iron, and a hammock slung between two trees. The sun was shining from the south and it filtered through the leaves, giving direct sunlight without any heat. The backyard was small and it dropped off into the Don River Valley.

The wonders of the city never stop, Frank thought.

"It is quite nice; I feel very fortunate," said Sloan.

"Yes, you are," Frank said and turned to look at the hammock.

"Would you like some iced tea?" he asked.

"I don't want you to go out of your way."

"It's nothing. I just made some. I'll go and get it." Sloan went through the door and was back quickly with a tray. He set it down on the table and motioned for Frank to sit down. He did. He filled a glass, passed it to Frank, and pointed to the cookies.

"Have a cookie. My mother made them," he said with a laugh. Frank laughed, although he didn't understand the joke.

"I think that I'm the only man in his sixties whose mother still makes him cookies," he said.

"Geez," said Frank, "you weren't kidding."

"Not at all. My mother calls me daily. To this day she slips me a few dollars every time I visit. She always supported my choice to become an artist even though the rest of my family was against it. She fought my father and grandfather until she won. Was and still is a grand and tough lady. But, she never understood that I had actually achieved some acclaim in the art world. If that means anything. She could never understand that I had become commercially successful."

"And she keeps giving you money?" asked Frank.

"As if she never felt I had a chance. So, she gives me what she can so that I can buy some groceries or take a nice girl out on a date." Sloan laughed hard at that, then took a drink of his iced tea. Frank noticed something about the man. There was a young quality to his face. He seemed unburdened.

"Oh, that is good. It is missing something, though." He ran into the house and quickly returned with a bottle of gin. He poured a large amount in his glass and took a drink.

"Ahhh, that's better. Now, why would you like to talk to me? I phoned a couple of people I know at your paper and they told me you weren't involved in the cultural side of things. What can I help you with? Can I offer you a little kick to your tea?" he added, holding the bottle up to Frank.

"No thanks," said Frank. "I'd like to discuss an old friend of yours by the name of Hayes."

Sloan's eyes became intense. He straightened up in his chair. Frank felt that he was being studied, figured out. There was an awkward silence.

"Well, Ford Hayes?" Sloan said with a smile. "You had better have a drink." He poured a large amount of gin into Frank's glass. Frank felt a sudden urge and took a long slow gulp.

Sloan stretched his legs and leaned back in his chair. It looked uncomfortable to Frank. The chair was iron and stiff. Sloan seemed relaxed, though. He closed his eyes and was silent for a moment. Frank looked at his drink and waited.

"Hayes and I were friends back at the College. That was during the war. He was a magnificent young man." Sloan drifted off into the past and was quiet. Frank felt flush. Had Hayes been a homosexual? Was Sloan his lover? Frank wondered what it might have been like to be gay in a group of people who found showing affection difficult even in heterosexual company.

"We were close back then," Sloan continued, "We did everything together. I was a bit of a sidekick to him, really. He wouldn't allow me to be everything to him." He looked at Frank coyly. Hayes was heterosexual. That was to let Frank know.

"Back then, the school was a very different place than it is today. It was far more exclusive but also less a thing of status to be enrolled there. Ford and I went through the entire time together. Well, almost the entire time."

"We went to university together and then..." Sloan finished his drink and then filled his glass with straight gin. "Then, he disappeared, for the first time. We weren't really ever friends again."

Frank realized that he had brought up the name of Sloan's first, unrequited love. Hayes must have meant everything to Sloan, perhaps since they were boys. It was a memory filled with joy and sadness. Sloan had buried it. He had gone on with his life and become successful, while Hayes had died and was forgotten. Now Frank had whispered a name into his ears that he probably wished to never hear again. Frank was used to that. Questioning people whose loved ones didn't make it out of a burning house. Or talking to parents of children who had disappeared and then asking to borrow a picture for the front cover. It was part of his job. He didn't like it any more than those who despised him for it. But he had come to realize that deep down, in a dark place filled with fear, hatred, and anger, the public wanted to see that photo. They wanted to read what the parents said, how they felt when the body was found. Frank had often thought that pain and agony made people feel more human. Even if that pain was someone else's.

Sloan began again. Frank sat quietly, deciding to speak only if Sloan got too far off track. He was sure that Sloan knew the path he was taking. He wouldn't stray. There was an excitement in Frank. Hayes had come to him without notice or desire like the dream on the subway train. He hovered over him and set off reactions in his brain. He felt that all he had to do was let Sloan talk and he would lead Frank to some unknown destination that he had been moving toward since the day on the dock at Jonathan's cottage. The pieces had fallen together from that day. All the wires that were normally crossed, the ones that threw everyone's life into a tangle of events and circumstances had seemed to be plugged in with some sort of order. One by one the electrical sparks had illuminated his way. Now he was plugged into Sloan.

"Ford and I lived close to one another when we were kids. His parents knew my parents, but they didn't like each other much. Old money doesn't always like old money. Worse yet was that my mother was French Canadian. That wasn't liked much around here in those days.

"Ford would come and call on me and then we'd walk to school together. That went on for ten years.

"He was an extraordinary young man. The smartest, bravest, most athletic, most creative person out of the whole bunch. That meant he wasn't well liked. You know, life isn't like in the movies. The best don't always rise to the top. Often times, their will is crushed by those less than them before they truly have a chance to shine. It is a horrible thing.

"The man who owns your newspaper was one of the boys who despised Ford. Stone would have given anything to smash Hayes to bits. I guess it's typical of boys at that age.

"But that didn't happen to Ford. He had a confidence and ability to make them all tremble in their shoes if he wanted. He could out-talk and out-think them. If he had to, and he did at times, he out-fought them. With all of that came deep resentment. He was hated by almost everyone in the place. Even the Masters didn't like him much. I'm sure you know how it was there. Men of great promise settling for what they consider lesser positions as teachers. Some were bitter. Many were angry. Ford would come into class and deflate their long and misguided lectures about philosophy or history or art. The whole school was afraid of him. I remember old Standford. Poor bastard began to cut apart some such subject with the wit of a butter knife. Ford listened for a while. I think we were discussing the British Empire or something. Standford was talking about the greater glory of our British legacy. Ford raised his hand. It made Standford stop for a second. He ignored Ford, but Ford sat there calmly with his hand raised. Standford almost began to panic. He turned his back to the class and continued. Christ I can almost hear him right now. 'And with the moral weight of British civilization, the Indian people began to take to the entire culture that have been transported from that green and gentle land.' When he turned back around, Ford was looking right at him with his hand in the air. Standford was furious. He went to his desk, slammed the book that lay open on it closed and dismissed the class.

"He was called to see the principal for that. Do you believe it?" Sloan shook his head and took a drink of gin. He motioned to Frank to do the same and Frank did so obediently.

"What was he going to say?" asked Frank.

"I don't know and I guess it doesn't really matter. The fact is, he could do it by just raising his hand," said Sloan.

Frank noticed the artist's speech beginning to slur. His eyes were closed, and it seemed as though sleep were upon him.

"Tell me about when Hayes was thrown out of school. Was it because of the incident with the Jewish boy?" Sloan shot up and he looked angrily at Frank. Sloan's eyes were piercing. Frank saw his expression, calm before, turn into something else. He was intrigued.

"You're a clever man, Frank," he said, raising an eyebrow. "Where did you hear about him being thrown out? Did the school tell you that?"

"Well, no. I got that from another source," said Frank feeling as though he should protect Gillis, although he didn't know why.

"First of all, your source is wrong. Let's start with that," said Sloan, straightening in his chair and brushing his hair back with his hands. "Ford left. They didn't throw him out. And yes, it was because of that incident. He was right, Hayes, I mean. That was why he had to leave. Do you understand that? He was right, and the rest of them, the Dean, the Masters, and especially Stone, they were wrong and that's why they wanted him to leave. Do you understand?" he asked Frank again. It made

Frank unsure. Did he really understand? He wouldn't have thought twice about leaving his high school. It didn't make sense to Frank. Sloan knew it.

He continued, "Ford wasn't like any other person. I have never met anyone like him. He was smart, strong, and brash. That was true. Those things were, in the eyes of people like those at the College, his parents, and the world, excusable. His biggest fault was something that they would not tolerate. It was the greatest sin to those pious, self-righteous bastards. It was that he was right. That was it. He was right about what he did with the young Jewish boy. He was right about bringing down the masters when they allowed themselves to become pompous. He was right about everything. That was his greatest sin. Do you understand? How could you? I'm sorry to say it, Frank, but you couldn't understand. Ford was cursed with clear thought. But that is true of so many people in this world. That is acceptable. What Ford also possessed, the thing that went against their old-world, blind, dogmatic order was that he also had humanity and compassion. Those two abilities together are difficult for people to bear. When he looked them in the face, and he always did, to tell them that they were wrong, they all knew that they were. They knew that they were standing in front a person who was their better. That is the one thing that they could not tolerate. Particularly when it is imposed upon them. When they stared into Ford's eyes, they were the first to blink each time. The incident with the Jewish boy was a chance for them to put an end to his tyranny over them. That's how they saw it, I'm sure. To them he was a tyrant of truth. They had him. Late in his final year at school, they felt that they could force him into compliance. He would have to subjugate himself to them or they would toss him out. Oh, they had no clue that they were doing that. How could they? Their minds had been closed for some time. They didn't know that they were there to break Ford, to make him tow their line. They felt they were there to enforce some sort of code of behaviour he had breached. They thought themselves thinkers and people who respected those who sought the truth. But they weren't and they didn't even know that and because they weren't, Ford had them beat.

"They called a school council on that day. We all were there, sitting in the chapel. The Dean sat on the stage with the Masters in their robes. Oh God, there was a sinister mood in the place. Everyone knew what had happened. Stone had been so mortified by the whole thing that he made sure that everyone heard about Hayes' behaviour. Stone, that cheat, that coward. After we were all in, Hayes walked in followed by two of the Junior Masters. He moved slowly to the stage and stood in front of them. The Dean stood. He was a tall man, but standing in front of Ford, he looked huge. He was about to speak when Ford cut him off. He spoke in a loud and clear voice. Christ, I remember that day as if I were still there. It caught the Dean off guard. 'Dean, Masters and fellow students. If it is your apology that you are about to offer me, then I accept. If I do not receive an apology, I will be forced to leave this school.' The place was silent. One of the Masters, an old English son of a bitch who hated Ford, stood but the man couldn't say anything. You have to remember that no student brought before the school council ever spoke. They were there to be punished. Ford stuck it to them and said, to hell with you boys in your black robes." Sloan's eyes smiled. Frank imagined that Sloan was playing that moment over in his head.

Frank didn't know what to think at this point. He had only heard about the young schoolboy. So what? There were grander things to be accomplished. Why should there be such a fuss about this boy? Was it his disappearance? Frank was still intrigued about why he got up and left on that day. The way he did it, not telling anyone, then showing up again a year and a half later. Where the hell did he go? What the hell did he do? Frank looked over at Sloan. He was slumped down in his chair again, his eyes closed. Was he asleep or just in some daydream about Hayes?

"Where did he go?" Frank said without getting Sloan's attention. "When he disappeared, where did he go?" Sloan didn't respond right away. Frank let the question hang in the afternoon breeze for a minute. He looked out onto the valley below. The highway that ran through it was closed for repairs. People were out of town on vacation, at their cottages, or playing golf. The flowerbeds in the garden gave off a sweet smell. Frank thought that he could be in the country somewhere, miles away from Toronto. How nice it was for Sloan to be able to hide here in the city. That was what he was doing on this little street tucked away in Cabbagetown. He was hiding. For some reason it bothered Frank. He didn't understand why.

"He went travelling. I think that is what it is called today. I think we may have called it something else. Discovering the world perhaps," said Sloan in a low voice. Frank looked over at him. His eyes were still shut. Frank waited for him to continue but he didn't.

"Where?" asked Frank.

"He didn't tell me," said Sloan slouching more in his chair, getting himself more comfortable. "He was thin as hell though when he came back, and his skin was dark, very tanned. Somewhere tropical I guess. What's it matter really. When he returned, well, needless to say, there was a bit of surprise."

"That's an understatement," said Frank.

"He wasn't a changed man or anything like that. In fact, when he got back, he was more himself than he had ever been. It was as though he was able to throw off the last bit that kept him connected to the rest of us and that allowed him to be who he was meant to be.

"That is the most difficult thing. To be yourself. I can only imagine the huge commitment that it was to be completely yourself, your inspired self. In my art, I look for that. I try to be myself and express only what I need to, but that might happen only once a year. That is the great work, the important work. Once a year I might be able to achieve that. Hayes walked around accomplishing it with every breath, every hand gesture, every smile."

Frank thought about it. That was what Sloan wanted. Frank thought about his own career. He thought about his horrible week as a columnist. He was still waiting to be happy with something he'd written. He wondered if it would ever happen. What would it be like to be without the notion of failure, without any second thoughts? To look at the world through crystal eyes, clear, precise, without fault. It was spiritual. That's what Sloan was saying. Had Hayes found that mythical knowledge of self? What was Frank thinking? Hayes was no prophet.

"Why did he leave?" asked Frank. A smile came across Sloan's face.

"Ahh, the why. How, when, where, why, what, and who. Those are the important details for you newspaper types. I suppose you call yourselves journalists now, don't you?"

"No," said Frank. "We call ourselves reporters."

"Of course you do. So, you want to know the why? Well, the why requires more gin." He moved up out of his awkward position in the chair. He went into the house and left Frank alone on the patio.

When Sloan returned with another bottle of gin, Frank noticed the sway in his step. He was drunk, and so was Frank. Sloan stopped in the middle of the patio and closed his eyes. He took a deep breath and a smile came to his face. He was smelling the sweet scent of the garden flowers in full bloom. Frank couldn't help but think of Hayes. Why had he left? What would that accomplish? Did he think that he would find some sort of comfort out there, wherever he went?

Sloan sat down. "I see I have you thinking, young Frank," said Sloan, pouring more liquor into their glasses. "Don't, for I shall now reveal all to you. The why is what you seek, my young friend, and now you will be given it on a platter. Are you ready?" Sloan looked at Frank, tilted his glass to him, and said, "cheers."

"Well, after Sloan left the College, his father decided that he had had enough of his son's misbehaviour. That was what he called it. It took some doing for him to get Ford into the university. But, being both an old boy himself and involved with the board they granted his son admission. From that day on, Ford's every move was watched by his father. He had to report to him on a daily basis. His father would review his studies and have regular conversations with his professors.

"But soon, Hayes became bored with the limited teachings at university. They weren't limited for those of us who were average students. In fact, they were quite challenging for me. But Ford began to lose interest. Even debating his professors wasn't interesting enough. Ford found them every bit as slow-witted as the Masters at college. So, he began to write.

"His first book was a small volume of poetry that was published by a friend of his father's. They were mainly about love and sold only because people who knew the name Hayes were curious to see what it was all about. Ford began to enjoy the fame. He was asked to speak to different clubs and organizations and there were a lot of readings at the family home when the Hayes' were entertaining. What he found most interesting about the experience was that for some reason women were intrigued by him. He told me once that the reason he would go to the functions was because there was usually some young female there who was willing to lose herself to an author. Soon, the only reason he read was for the sexual conquest of it all.

"In his second year as an undergraduate, he wrote a short novel that was again published by the publishing house of his father's friend. This book was received with far less enthusiasm than the first, although some critics thought it to be a true piece of literary art. The problem was that Ford had used many of his father's friends as thinly disguised characters. An account of a group of Toronto businessmen who engaged in all sorts of debasing acts. It was just a little racy for Protestant Toronto. The snotty group that had bought his previous book wouldn't touch this one. There was even a discussion in the Toronto city council to ban it.

"That didn't matter to Ford. He became increasingly interested in drinking and sexual encounters with women of its liberal literary community, of which he was now a celebrated member. As he continued his studies – his father made sure of that – he would sleep with every woman who would have him. That was all well and good until some of Toronto's most well-known debutantes came up pregnant. The joke was that there was a Swiss clinic that knew Ford by name. Of course, that was all gossip.

"It wasn't until his final year that Ford came out with his third book. He had already been accepted into law school and was only waiting to graduate. This was another book of poetry. A rambling litany of words which seemed to have no beginning and no end. No publisher in Toronto would touch it. A small New York publishing house, one that specialized in religious books, finally put it in print. The few copies that were circulated in Canada caused quite a stir. Hayes mentioned people by name and spoke of them in the most unflattering terms. Calls came into the Hayes house from friends and parents of daughters. The older Hayes was livid and, I suppose, felt he had allowed his son's behaviour to go on too long.

"One day Ford was summoned by his father's driver. The driver made sure that he got properly dressed and drove him down to the Monarch Life Insurance building. Hell, that was a grey old piece of crap. Even the Heritage Society was happy to see that torn down when they built Mount Sinai Hospital. Hayes was met at the front door of the building by a man, not much older than he was, who escorted him to the executive suites where his father's office was. He had to sit down in the reception area as one of the secretaries went to inform his father that he was there. After waiting for some time, the same young man ushered him into his father's office and closed the door behind him. There Hayes saw his mother standing beside his father's desk, with the older Hayes sitting, reading some papers. His mother smiled meekly as his father waved him to a chair without even looking up. His father scribbled his signature on the bottom of the last page of what he had been reading and buzzed for the secretary to come in. The door opening again apparently made his mother jump slightly and she spoke to Hayes to cover her nervousness. I suppose she asked him how he was or something else as the old man gave instructions to the woman he had summoned. Then, she took the papers and left leaving Hayes with his parents. That's when the old man stood up behind his desk.

"Now Frank, it's important to let you know that the older Hayes was a tall man, thin with yellow skin and silver hair. He had a low growl of a voice." Sloan took a drink from his glass. The image Frank conjured made him feel sick.

"The old man waved his hand to stop Hayes and his mother from speaking. That's when he let Ford know where he stood. I can hear him saying it now. 'Son,' he must've said, 'your mother and I have decided that your behaviour is to stop. There is no point in trying to deny who and what you are. Things are expected of you. This family will not be let down. We did not have a son to see him act in this way. From now on there will be no more writing, no more women and no more embarrassments. In this your mother and I are in agreement.' The elder Hayes smiled. That's what Ford told me, he really hadn't seen his father smile much but at that moment, he smiled and leaned down behind his desk and pulled out a parcel. His mother smiled too and then Ford's father handed him the parcel and motioned for him to open it. It was a stack of law books. Inside each was Ford's name, neatly inscribed with the date. At that point pleasantries were probably exchanged and Ford most likely kissed his mother's cheek and left with the stack of books under his arm.

"That night, well after midnight, I heard a knock at my window. I was startled because my room was on the third floor.

Hayes had climbed a tree, gotten onto the roof, and then lowered himself onto the ledge by my room. I let him in and we smoked cigarettes until dawn. I had never seen him that way. He was deep within himself. He had wanted all his life to help change the world and his father had taken away every opportunity and forced him to become what was expected of him. He had deeper questions. It must have been devastating for him. He could have done anything, you know. He could have become one of the greatest people, well, in the way the world acknowledges its great people. He had that sort of ability and belief in himself. He saw things. The way things were and how they should be. He could sit for hours in the library or in his back yard or wherever he might be, and think about things. It was as if life, all of life, was within his grasp. And even though it was there, right there, he did not reach for it as most of us would have. He didn't need to try and attain it you see, because it was already his. In some ways, trying to understand him, to understand why he left and why he came back and then, well...we would have to change how we think to know that. We would have to think like Ford thought. We would have to go beyond the four walls of the room we live in and search beyond it. Ford used to say to me, and this was early in his life – when we were very young and well before any of those events that still seem to mark his life happened – that life follows you, wherever you are. As I get older that seems so simple. But that has always stuck with me. Why he left comes back to that really, doesn't it." Sloan stopped and took a drink.

"Now, all he had to look forward to was law school and taking over the family fortune. For him it wasn't enough. That next day, the first day of class, he took all those textbooks and his new brief, kissed his mother goodbye and left to go down to Osgoode Hall. No one saw him again for a year and a half but they found those books neatly stacked on the counter at the law school bookstore."

Frank looked perplexed, and a smile came across Sloan's

face and he laughed in a pleasant and comforting way that made Frank smile as well.

"The question to you, Frank, is: did he really leave anything?"

Hours later, Frank looked out at the lights from across the valley. He had a headache. The gin had gotten to him and he wished he had had a chance to sleep. Sloan had been asleep in the chair on his patio for over an hour. Frank waited for him to wake up. He would have to make a decision. It would be a difficult one, he knew that.

Frank walked back toward the patio. The night was hot. It hadn't cooled since mid-afternoon. His mouth was dry. He decided to go into the house and get a drink of water. He realized he should also call Willie. Frank thought about what Sloan had said. He had only seen Hayes twice after he reappeared. One time was a chance meeting along the street near their parents' homes, shortly after he had come back. Hayes barely remembered Sloan, or pretended not to remember. But how could he not remember? Sloan said that Hayes appeared smaller. He looked thin and pale. Sloan said that the way Hayes spoke was almost as though the conversation wasn't taking place. It was as though Hayes was thinking to himself. His words went in all directions. Then, without saying anything, Hayes left him standing. Sloan couldn't believe it. At first he had felt hurt by it. After thinking about it, Sloan had said he felt only fear for Hayes. What did that mean, fear for him?

He passed Sloan, who was snoring. Stepping inside he paused to let his eyes adjust to the darkness. He took a glass from the drying rack next to the sink. He turned the tap on and let it run for a moment, feeling the water with his finger. He put the glass under and let it fill. He took a long gulping drink. Some of the water spilled out the side and onto his face and shirt. He finished all the water and then filled it again. This time he took a slow sip and then turned to look for the phone.

There didn't seem to be one in the kitchen. He walked out towards the studio. The hall was dark. He stumbled along, trying not to spill his water. He felt the wooden board that ran along the wall. It was old and needed a new finish. Reaching along he felt the opening of the door to the living room studio. A street light shone and lit up the room enough for Frank to see where he was walking. He saw a desk up against the window. He thought he saw a phone on it. He walked over slowly so as not to step on the works of art in progress on the floor. He put his hand on the desk to steady himself and put the glass of water down, trying to find a spot amongst the clutter. He switched on the desk lamp. The light hurt his eyes. Behind him was a sea of blue canvasses and paint and stains and brushes. Frank felt like he was under water.

He squinted and twisted back toward the desk. The phone was there. Frank dialed Willie's number. The numbers had blue paint all over them. The phone was very modern and sleek-looking. It seemed very out of place with the rest of the decor. Perhaps Sloan couldn't avoid it and had to get his old phone replaced.

Frank got her answering machine. Perhaps she had gone out already. She was seeing her father on one of his rare appearances in Toronto. He wasn't in town or the country very often. Willie liked to see him alone so they could get caught up without distractions.

"Hi Willie, it's me, I'm still doing that interview, so I'll just meet you later. Bye." He hung up.

Sitting at the artist's desk, he looked out onto the street. One single light lit up the three houses. He thought again that it was incredible that, in a city as large as Toronto, there was a place like this in its very heart. Frank took a look at the table top. There were newspaper clippings, papers, and books all over it. He took a drink of water. He couldn't help himself. He began looking through the papers. There were bills for art supplies and other things like the phone and heating oil. Some were new but the heating oil bill was well past due. The books weren't very interesting. There was one on birds and another on decorating your city home. Perhaps Sloan was thinking of starting to paint with another colour. There were some other books that looked old and weathered, a dictionary and a personal telephone book. Frank decided against looking through that. Sloan was being very helpful, he didn't want to invade his privacy. There were two newspaper clippings. Frank recognized one. It was from *The Globe* from last Monday about the poor yuppie cottagers who couldn't find any water frontage and wanted some crown land opened up for them. The other clipping was a follow-up story that was from Wednesday's paper. It was a small blurb about a possible lawsuit being filed by the group that called itself Vacation Lands Opportunities Group. VLOG. What a bunch of idiots, thought Frank.

He looked down the front of the desk. There were only two drawers, on the right side. Frank pulled at the top one. There was nothing inside, just pens and some loose-leaf paper. That was all. The bottom drawer was larger. The lock looked well-used. There were three neat little files. He pulled the first out. Paid bills and bank accounts. He checked the numbers. Sloan was worth a fortune. Shit, thought Frank, this can't all be from his painting. Frank put the file back together and replaced it.

Frank took out the second file. It was just a couple of pages. It was a list of all his paintings, the originals and who owned them. There were about one hundred. Each one had the owner's name and what they paid. Some had a lot of entries, presumably from sale and resale of the same painting.

Frank returned that one and pulled out the last file. It was the thickest. All the papers were deeds to land. Shit, he thought, this guy owns some property. There had to be about thirty deeds. Frank checked the acreage. Each one was thousands of acres. Frank did a quick count. There had to be seventy thousand acres of land. He checked the postal codes. They all started with L, therefore they were outside of the city, which started with the letter M. This area had to be close. Newfoundland was A, Frank knew that. He always assumed that British Columbia was Z, although he suspected that his assumption may be wrong. Nonetheless, he thought that L had to be somewhere in Ontario. Frank thumbed his way through the properties. There weren't any purchase dates but the deeds all seemed very old. At the back of the file was a letter. Frank read it. The letter stated that Sloan had the right to act on behalf of Mrs. Yvonne Ashe in all land dealings. And that Mrs. Ashe would like to have the province control the land as crown land until her death, at which point the province would take over the land's ownership, to be used only as a provincial park. There were some further stipulations. There could be no cottagers or powerboats. No leases of land. No hunting, no fishing etc. It didn't sound as though it would be a place where people would want to go. Frank pictured Mrs. Ashe. She was some rich old woman who had outlived her children and didn't like her grandchildren much. Instead of giving them the land and having them sell it off, she would give it to the province to use. I bet she isn't well liked, thought Frank. Suddenly, he felt flushed. The blood rushed from his head, his heart was pounding so hard. He gulped down the rest of the water.

Sloan had moved from the chair to the hammock. He was swinging back and forth. The light of his cigarette was moving like a firefly. Frank walked over to him and stood by the hammock.

"Frank, where have you been?" asked Sloan.

"I was making a phone call," said Frank.

"That was some phone call. You didn't call Australia did you?" Sloan took a long drag. Frank noticed a different tone in his voice. He was short with him. It had been a long day now and Sloan had to be feeling the effects of all the alcohol.

"I just had to call someone. I didn't mean to be that long."

"Oh, were you long?" snapped Sloan. It startled him. Sloan continued to swing casually in the hammock.

"I was longer than I thought I would be," said Frank, retreating. He wanted to leave. Sloan was silent for a moment. Frank still hadn't heard about the other time Sloan had seen Hayes before he disappeared for the second time. He wasn't sure if he should ask or not.

Sloan broke the silence. "Frank, I like you," said the artist, trying to sound less hard. "I think that what you are trying to do is interesting but I think you should stop. Leave this thing alone. It isn't worth it." Frank didn't understand. What was Sloan saying? Why did he want Frank to stop? The pounding of his heart returned. The swing of the hammock was making him sick. He smelled the strong, sweet smoke from Sloan's cigarette.

"Why?" was all Frank could manage.

"Because, you are a young man and you have a future. Hayes was like you once. Perhaps it would have led him in the same direction as you. He once worked for *The Globe and Mail*, after his return. They wanted him to write on the arts, but he didn't have any answers for them. That's what people want, answers. All Hayes had were questions. He questioned everything. He couldn't stop himself. Even when he tried to fit in he couldn't. There was something inside him that wouldn't allow him to. It tormented him.

"There is no running from your questions. They remain with you. Questions expose others as well as yourself, even if you take great care. That is dangerous, young Frank. And that can cost those around you a great deal." Sloan paused. He was thinking.

"But those questions persist, Frank, and they can turn on you. Hayes was lucky enough to disappear when he did. The questions he asked were starting to turn on him. Why should you risk that, Frank? Why?"

Frank's head was pounding now, to the point where he couldn't think. He looked over at the small iron table. The gin bottle was still there. He thought about having another drink. That wouldn't help though. Sloan lit another cigarette.

"Frank, I come from a world that you don't understand. I know that you think you do but you don't. And the people in that world have a different way of looking at the most simple of things. Life seems larger to them than to you. I don't mean that as a slight, I am saying that not as a criticism of you but of them. For them, much is at stake with everything they do and because of it they guard themselves and, most importantly, who they are. I look at you, Frank, and I see someone who wears his life on his sleeve, so to speak. Every emotion, every thought there for the world to see. And, I would think that most people are like that and even many of the people I knew growing up were like that, at least at some point. But people like you, Frank, don't rule the world. I'm sorry to say it but I'm being honest. You don't take positions of true power. Those positions are held by people like the man who owns your paper. Harold Stone lacks all those things that make real people human. He walks about thinking of his place in history as though that matters. And it does. I can humbly say that I have a place in history now. That's due mostly to the misguided praise of my dabblings. Stone, though, believes that his place and his power are more than earned, they are deserved. He has created himself by the sheer force of who he is. A world conqueror. One of the chosen. Now think, if you will, what a man like that would do if someone could walk into his life tomorrow and change that. Take all that away from him by simply appearing from out of thin air, so to speak."

Sloan's eyes narrowed.

"See Frank, even now you don't realize what I'm saying. How could that happen to Stone, you might ask, a man of such wealth and power? Well, let me say this, that when you are in Stone's position you do worry because who you are depends on having that privilege, because without that privilege you would be nothing and could make nothing of yourself. When the name that you've said to me is mentioned in their presence, that is the fear that comes to them. It is cold and dark and real, like some ghost from a dark place."

Sloan smiled again at Frank as images filled the young man's head. Frank tried to speak.

"How..." he said, staggering through the word.

"You know, the thing I remember most about Ford," said Sloan, changing the subject while giving himself a push off the tree near the hammock to start it swinging again, "were his eyes. They were tremendous and vibrant. He got them from his mother. She was a warm person. Gentle and kind and loving. His father was a bastard. He had these steely grey eyes. The eyes of a man who knew no compassion. Only success. That was how he measured you. What you did and what you had and, more importantly, how you got it. Ford's mother was something else. She was also very nice to me. And Hayes loved her very much."

"I think I'll just go now," said Frank looking down as he turned, feeling that he had to watch his footing. "I hope that we can talk again sometime."

"Whenever you wish," said Sloan, letting the cigarette dangle from his mouth. Frank walked toward the door that led to the kitchen and then on to the front door.

"Frank?" Sloan called just as Frank was about to enter the doorway to the kitchen.

Frank turned to face him.

"I hope you found everything you had to."

Magnetic North

Chapter 8

They had left late. It was almost five o'clock before they got onto the highway. Willie had seen her father the evening before and had gotten home late. Frank told her what Sloan had said. They talked until early that morning. Frank didn't know what he should do. Neither did Willie. Eventually, they decided to go look for a ghost.

The road north wasn't crowded on a Sunday evening. The terrain along the highway was made up of rolling farm land. At the crest of hills, Frank could look out over the dark, rich earth for miles. In the distance, he could see houses, barns, and silos standing in small clumps. How wonderfully lonely they seemed, washed in an orange glow. Large rolls of hay were scattered in fields, like great balls left on a golden playground. Their shadows lay behind them, tired from a hot August day.

Just past Barrie the scenery changed. Blue water and thick green trees replaced the neatly kept acreage. As Frank looked over the water on both sides of the highway he could see the white hulls of power boats streaming across the surface, leaving long lines of foam as markers. On the road south was a line of cars. Cottagers spilling into the city after having crept out of it on Friday afternoon. The cars flew by, going well over the speed limit. Along the side of the road, at gas stations and restaurants, tanned people in neon shorts and baseball caps sat talking and laughing. Stands selling wild berries were filled with those wanting to take the taste of the country back to the city. They haggled over the price with the sellers. Young men and women stood posing one last time for their companions. They laughed hard, clutching arms and shoulders, touched by an inner sense of connection. It was a connection to the land and to the people that they were with. It was a connection that came from within. The need to stand for something, to be something and make a place in a world that was busy ripping itself apart. Away from the crowded streets, commuter trains, and rush hour traffic, people could laugh and talk freely. Frank looked at them as if he owned his empty side of the highway.

Willie was asleep. He looked at her hands, folded neatly in her lap. Her head lay back on the seat. It had been a hard decision to make, leaving behind her commitments and travelling north with Frank. In fact, it was Willie who had pushed for them to go. She felt that Frank needed to follow whatever instincts he had. It was up to him to satisfy his curiosity. There was no need to worry about his job. Jobs came and went. His life was more than any job. She didn't want him bothered by a ghost in the trees for the rest of his life. Although she was serious when she told him this, Frank had smiled. He couldn't hide it. She'd smiled too. They knew now, both of them, what they had suspected for some time. Although they never spoke of it, it would often come up in that sort of way. One of them would speak about the future and the other would join in, knowing without question that they had a stake in each other. That the other's life was, in fact, now and forever, part of theirs. It always made them feel good. They felt attached to one another. That feeling of belonging was one that was undeniably comforting. They never spoke of marriage, except once when Willie told Frank that she was against it. The ceremony was something she desperately wanted to avoid, for many reasons, but mostly because growing up her life had been full of ceremony but with little meaning. The times she had asked her parents, almost begged them, to explain the reasons behind certain things – dressing for Sunday dinner, or why they had to always leave their father alone when he first got home from work – her curiosity was met with a stern response. These times seemed trivial when she looked back at them now, but they had shaped her notion of society's need for ceremony. She shuddered when she thought about the grand affair her mother would force on her if she and Frank got married. Best to just avoid it altogether.

When Frank called Carl at home in the morning and told him Frank nearly passed out from the tension. He was putting his job, already tenuous, in more jeopardy. What the hell did he think he was doing? People were unemployed everywhere and here he was pushing his luck. Frank thought about telling his parents. They certainly wouldn't understand what he was doing. They were glad that he was working. Leaving a good job with benefits? Frank couldn't even imagine what they would think. But Carl wasn't angry. He seemed to understand. It would be a vacation, or if necessary, a leave of absence. "If you need me, call," he had said. There was comfort in that.

Willie stirred beside him, trying to regain a comfortable position. They were coming up on Huntsville. It was about 8:30, and he was hungry. Instead of having lunch, they had been busy calling people and changing appointments. Willie had to track down a partner at a golf course. That wasn't such a bad thing. He was the type of guy who liked to be on his cellular phone. It made him feel as though he was part of the action. He wasn't happy that Willie couldn't make it into work. He told her that she had to be back by Tuesday morning. When she hung up, she looked upset. Frank tried to convince her to stay and go to work. She wouldn't think of it. She was glad to be going. It didn't matter that she didn't quite understand what was driving Frank. She just wanted to be with him, alone, away from everything.

"You want some dinner?" asked Frank.

She smiled and closed her eyes. She looked content.

"Yeah, let's stop somewhere."

"How about Huntsville? Do you want to pull in there?"

"Sure," she said.

Driving into the resort town on a Sunday night was like walking into the aftermath of a party. The place, devoid of people for the most part, had the evidence of some sort of merriment strewn over it from corner to corner. The sun was setting and shades of purple and orange lit up the sky. Frank turned the car into The Boat House Restaurant. The place seemed deserted.

"Geez, The Boathouse," said Willie. "I've been here before." Her voice was filled with memories.

"Camp days?" said Frank, turning off the ignition.

"Camp days," she said, echoing him. He leaned over and kissed her on the lips. She put her hand on the back of his head. He pulled his head away and smiled at her. She was sleepy. Her eyes weren't fully opened.

Frank took Willie's hand in his.

There were a few people in some of the booths and a couple at the bar talked to the bartender. The decor was mostly wood, rough cut and unfinished. A line of booths ran all the way around the perimeter, leaving openings for the doors to the washrooms and kitchen. The bar was between the two sets of doors and seemed a little out of place. There were a few other tables scattered on an elevated area in the middle of the room. They looked down on a dance floor that was probably busy on Friday and Saturday nights.

The waitress brought Willie and Frank to booth in the far corner, well-removed from the other guests. Frank wondered if they weren't sending off some sort of signal. Maybe they looked as though they needed to be alone.

"Can I get yas somethin' from the bar?" said the girl. She

was young for someone who seemed so world-weary.

Willie's eyes were still a little glassy. She smiled at him.

"I'll have a draft," she said.

"Me too," added Frank.

"Sure thing," said the girl and she spun on one heel and went back to the bar. Frank heard the twang of country voices but it was too low to identify the singer. He picked up one of the menus that the waitress had left. Willie did the same.

The waitress came back and put the glasses of beer down in front of them.

"I'll give yas a little while longer to decide, okay?" she said.

"Great," said Frank, smiling at her. He realized he was trying very hard to be pleasant. Willie was staring out the window at the lake that the town was built around. The night sky made it rich and dark blue. A few boats raced across the far end with all of their running lights on.

"Nice, isn't it?" said Frank.

The waitress returned.

"What'll yas have?" she asked.

"Two cheeseburgers with fries and gravy," said Willie, ordering for both of them.

"Ok," said the waitress scribbling down the order. She took the menus and went into the kitchen.

"It's been a long time since I was here," said Willie.

"Yeah? When was the last time?" He was glad that she was talking.

"I'm not sure, but it was a while ago," she said. "We used to come here when we were counsellors at camp. Every Friday night we'd get into the old truck that they let us use for supply runs and we'd head into town."

"What an adventure," said Frank, drinking his beer. He put the glass back on the table and moved it in little circles through the condensation it left.

"We thought so," said Willie. "We would come into town and flirt with the counsellors from the boys' camps and come in here and drink underage. We thought we were rebels." She stopped for a moment and looked out at the dying light across the lake. She smiled broadly and let out a laugh. "Christ, we were such little girls. You know, it's funny. When you're that age you can't help but feel that every emotion, every decision, every thought you have is important. It means so much." She looked over at Frank. He nodded, thinking back to those summer days he spent with his friends, lost in the heat and the lazy days of youth.

"Most of the time I look back at those days and they seem like, I don't know, like some story I read or something. It's as if they never happened. Like I had been watching someone's life on TV. But I come back to these places, or smell something, or hear a song and it takes me right back to where I was when I first experienced it. There I am at camp or at school. I'm in class or kissing some guy..."

"Hey, wait a minute. Kissing someone else?" Frank broke in.

"Shut up, would you? I'm the one chasing a ghost now." She took a drink of beer. Frank smiled. "I mean," she continued, "I mean, it's funny to think that I felt that way once. I felt it with absolutely everything I had. Geez, I remember sitting in that booth behind you. Cameron Taylor kissed me and I nearly ripped my clothes off I was so turned on."

"I'm not sure I like where this is going," said Frank. Willie continued ignoring him.

"Cameron Taylor." She slid down into the seat, her body shaking as she laughed.

"Yes, Willie," said Frank in a patronizing tone. "Let it out. That's right, honey, it's good for you." Willie sat up and wiped her tears.

"Cameron Taylor was such a goof and I was ready to give it all to him. If he wasn't such a goofy kid, he could have taken me down by the lake and I would have done anything he wanted."

"I'm not sure I want to hear any more of this," said Frank. He waved to the waitress.

They drove around the small town and decided on a motel near the highway. Frank parked the car while Willie went to check in. When Frank walked into the lobby with their small bag, Willie had just finished filling out the registration card. There were only two rooms left in the motel. They had forgotten that it was the height of the tourist season. A group of Japanese had taken most of them. They had come to take in the scenery and play golf on one of the many courses becoming more and more common in the area. As Willie and Frank walked through to their room they saw the smiling faces of Japanese children running from room to room. Their parents stood in the halls talking to one another. The men smoked strong cigarettes and there was a cloud in the hall because of it. As Willie and Frank passed them, they smiled and gave small bows. Their opened doors revealed even more people talking and enjoying themselves. Sounds were coming from everywhere. Smiles came from the rooms to Frank and Willie.

When they got to their room and got inside they both laughed. It was hard not to. It was a fun atmosphere in the hall that they had just walked through. Frank threw the bag on the bed. The room was typically low-budget. Two double beds and a small table with two chairs, a TV set on a chest of drawers, a few lamps and a night table with a clock radio between the beds. Everything was securely fastened to the piece of furniture it sat on.

Willie sat down on the far bed, took off her shoes, and threw them on top of the small table. Frank walked over to the bathroom and turned on the light.

"Nice clean bathroom," he said to himself more than to Willie. "I think I'll take a shower," he called out to Willie.

"I'll join you," said Willie. She walked toward the small table and took off her watch, her bracelet, her necklace, and put them down. She took off her top and her bra and put them on the bed with the bag. She took off her earrings and put them in the pocket of her shorts. Then she took off her shorts and underwear and threw them on the bed as well. Frank turned the water on and let the water run over his hand, adjusting the temperature. He took his shirt off and hung it on the back of the bathroom door. He took off his pants and his boxer shorts and put them over the shirt.

Willie walked into the bathroom and pushed past Frank. She stuck her hand in the shower to feel the temperature of the water.

"It's too cold," she said as she reached down to increase the hot water. As she leaned forward, Frank looked at her breasts hanging down. He thought it was funny that breasts could seem so utterly erotic at one time and so absolutely strange at another. He looked down at his penis. Christ, that has got to look weird to her, he thought.

"Do you get turned on when you see my penis?" he asked Willie. She continued to try and get the mix of water just right.

"No," she said in what seemed to Frank to be a very matter-of-fact way. "Why, do you?" she mocked. Frank frowned.

"Oh, don't worry," she said in a motherly voice while stepping over to him and caressing him. "It's a very nice penis." She moved away from him and stepped into the shower. He followed her in. They both stood for a while and let the water run down their bodies. Frank took up the small bottle of shampoo and opened the cap.

"Mm, kiwi," he sniffed the fruity odour. "Pretty high-class for a two-star hotel." He put some of the shampoo in his hand and began to wash his hair. Willie took the bottle from him and did the same. She closed her eyes and began to rub the shampoo into her hair, creating a white foamy lather.

"What do you plan on doing, now that you've come up here?"

"I don't know," he said. He let Willie rinse her hair and then shut off the water. Willie pulled the shower curtain open. She took one of the neatly folded towels and handed it to Frank. Then she took one for herself. They both shook them open and began to dry themselves.

"After you leave in the morning, I think I'll drive up to Jon's cottage and walk around."

"The woods aren't someplace you'll want to wander around in by yourself. You can get lost very easily. Are you sure you'll be all right?" said Willie, bending over and letting her hair hang as she dried it.

"I'll be all right," said Frank. They had talked about this the night before. Willie had gone over all the scenarios and told him story after gruesome story about the danger he could be getting himself into.

"You've told me what I should do and I'll do it. I don't want to get lost any more than you want me to. Or am I assuming too much?"

Willie rolled her eyes and didn't answer. She stepped out of the tub and wrapped the towel around her chest. She took a smaller folded towel and shook it loose. She continued to dry her hair. She turned and looked at Frank for a moment.

"Frank, what will you do, you know, if you find him?" Then she rolled her eyes. "What the hell am I saying?" she said, and walked out of the bathroom and sat on one of the beds. She turned the TV on and started going through the channels. Frank stepped out of the tub. He thought for a minute about the question. It seemed odd now that someone had said it. He sat beside her on the bed.

"I don't know," he said. He knew that she had faith in him but it was hard to believe what he had told her. He didn't really believe it fully. Could Hayes be alive somewhere in the forest? It seemed impossible. "All I know is that there has been too much said over the last week for me to simply say 'Wow, what a story,' and leave it at that. I don't know if I want this to be true or if I want this to just be a ridiculous little trip. Maybe it will give me a kick, get me going again. Maybe that's why I'm up here. Maybe life has already become too much for me and I need some sort of diversion. Oh shit, Willie. I'm not sure of anything now."

There was a quiet moment between them. Willie looked at him and smiled. She leaned her head on his shoulder. Her wet hair on his skin reminded him of the weekend before, the day he'd seen that strange figure on that secluded lake. Willie had always been the thing Frank could come back to. She'd centred him from the day they had first met. Now, she was telling him to go and seek out an answer to something that was deeper than the fate of Cecil Rutherford Hayes. Perhaps she was really sending him to find out something about himself. It was that idea which scared him most.

Chapter 9

"Hello?" grumbled Frank. "Hello?" he said again, clearing his throat. There was no answer. He looked over at the digital clock next to the bed. It was an automated wake up call. Willie didn't stir. Frank walked over to the window. He pulled the drapes open enough to look out. The Japanese were all standing around their buses, dressed to play golf. They stood in groups of five or six as they took pictures. Everyone was laughing and most of the men were smoking cigarettes. The children sat on the grass beside the parking lot. There weren't as many of them as Frank had estimated last night. Two of the women sat on the grass with them. A small Japanese woman in a uniform walked from group to group and they started to board the bus. As she left each group she gave a slight bow. She must be the tour guide, thought Frank.

"Frank," said Willie from the bed.

"Yeah?" Frank said, turning around. He saw Willie hadn't moved.

"Why are you up?" she asked, still not moving.

"I've got a lot to do, and you have to get going back to the city," Willie let out a groan.

"Don't make me go back," she said, finally turning to look at him.

"You've got to go. You're spoiling someone's golf game being here and you know how lawyers hate their golf games to be spoiled. It's close to becoming unconstitutional." Willie didn't laugh. She looked at him and he realized that though she might have been joking about not going back, she would actually rather be with him. He walked over to the bed and sat down.

"Hey, one of us has to keep their job, you know?" he said, stroking her hair. "It might as well be you."

"Do you think they'll fire you for this?" She moved over to him and wrapped her arms around his waist and put her head in his lap.

"They don't fire people any more. They'll just release me from my contractual obligation in order to downsize and become more competitive for the new global economy." Frank stroked Willie's hair. She wasn't laughing. He didn't know how to reassure her. He probably would be fired for what he was doing. He had the leave time available, but the fact was that he had been warned, twice, not to pursue this particular story. That didn't just come from his editor but also the publisher and, more importantly, the owner. His position with the paper was all but over. Unless, of course, he came back with nothing. Then perhaps, if he explained things to Carl in the right way, he might be able to resume his job. He thought about that for a moment. The idea of resuming what he was doing wasn't exactly what he wanted either.

He moved off her lap and toward the window. The bus outside had gone. "The Japanese tourists have gone off to play golf," he said. "Let's have breakfast."

Afterwards, they drove around town until they found a car rental agency. Frank got a car for three days. He didn't know if he would need it longer, but the college student who did the paperwork told him that he would be able to extend it if he had to. Another boy, probably not out of high school, drove it from the back parking lot to where they were standing. It wasn't much of a car. Frank had to walk around it with the boy and was informed of all the dents they knew about and that he would be responsible for any new ones they found when it was returned. They checked the mileage and the amount of gas in the tank together. Frank was given the keys.

Willie was sitting in her car by the time Frank and the boy had finished. He walked over to her and leaned in the window.

"I guess I'll go now," she said. She seemed sad.

"Okay," said Frank, feeling the same way.

"I don't get it," said Willie, looking up at Frank. Tears began to well up in her eyes. "Why am I so upset about this?" She wiped the first tear from her eyes.

"I don't know," said Frank.

"I feel as though we're breaking up or something; it's crazy," said Willie, trying to make her voice sound firm.

"Come on, Willie. You know that I love you," He felt as if he was pleading with her to take him back, to give him one more chance.

"I know, I love you too. But it, oh, I don't know. I'd better just go," she said, then started the car.

"Listen," said Frank, touching her arm and then putting his hand on the back of her head. "I'll call you in a week and tell you what I've found. But remember, I'm coming back," Frank couldn't help but think that he sounded like he was someone in an old war movie. *I'll be back, don't worry, but now, I've got a job to do.* She smiled. He leaned in and kissed her.

"Okay," she said, wiping her nose with her hand. "I'll be home in about four hours and then I think I'm just going to sit on my balcony and look out onto the lake."

"Are you going to count the hours until I return?" asked Frank.

"I'll count them until I fall asleep," she said. They kissed again. Willie put the car in gear and pulled out into the street that led to the highway. Frank walked back to his car. The boy was in the corner of the lot, with another car that had just come back.

"Which way to the municipal office?" Frank called to him.

"What?" asked the boy blankly.

"The courthouse. Which way to the courthouse?" The boy thought for a moment.

"Head back to Main Street, toward the centre of town," he said. "You can't miss it, it has four pillars with a big staircase in front."

"Thanks."

"You in trouble or something?" asked the boy, adding together a tearful goodbye with a courthouse visit.

"Not yet," said Frank. He got into the car, shut the door, started it up and drove toward the centre of town.

Frank went to the records department at the courthouse; it also served as the licensing office. People who think government is bloated should spend the day in a small town courthouse, thought Frank. Workers doubled and tripled up on jobs. That was before they were forced to do that. Frank asked for land use maps for the areas north of the town. Hunstville was the only real population centre in a huge county that was made up mostly of cottages and some commercial mining. It had once been a thriving forestry region. Natural resources had been its lifeblood. With better and less expensive materials coming from other parts of the country and the world, the town had become not much more than a tourist stop on the way to whatever piece of land travellers might have in the area.

"Here you go," said the large woman behind the counter. She had on a pair of glasses with an out-of-style frame. The arms of the glasses connected at the bottom of the lens and had a curve in them to bring them up to the ear. She smiled at Frank.

"You can't take them out of the office. So if you'd like, you can sit over there and look at them." She pointed to a small desk with a chair in the corner. The desk was like one from a school. The chair was plastic. So much for the rustic charm, thought Frank. He took the book over to the desk and set it down.

Frank began to flip through the pages. He saw the numbered markings for the pieces of property. He was looking specifically for the map with lots that had deed numbers beginning with AC, the letters he saw at Sloan's home. He found the page and took out the piece of paper that he had in his wallet. It had the deed numbers of all the pieces of property owned by Mrs. Ashe that Sloan had in his file. Frank checked the first number and looked for it on the map. He put down his pen cap to mark it. He checked the next number and looked for it. It was well above the pen cap. He looked at the map and then at the numbers on his paper. He needed to get a copy he could write on. He picked up the book and went back to the counter.

"Excuse me?" he asked the woman, who was now at her desk.

"Yup?" she said, getting up and coming over to the counter. Frank saw how difficult her size made it for her to get up.

"Is there a chance I can get a copy of this?"

"Oh sure," she said, "But I'll have to charge ya five dollars. You got to give the government its share." She laughed and took the book back from him. She placed it on a large photocopier that sat humming in the corner. The book was still too big for the copier.

"I'll have to make two copies of this but I'll only charge ya for one, ok?" she said. She didn't wait for a response. The copier was very modern and looked out of place. She hummed as she put the lid down and pressed the button to make a copy. A large 11x17 copy of one half of the map came out and lay in the tray. She lifted the lid and moved the book so that the other side of the map was revealed. She put the lid down and pressed the button again. Another sheet came out and lay in the tray.

"You still need this book?" she asked Frank.

"No, the copies will be fine, thanks," he said. She took up

the book and took it into the back room where it came from. She came back and took up the two copies. She examined them and seemed satisfied. She walked over to her desk and got the Scotch Tape dispenser, and brought it and the maps over to the counter. Frank watched her as she placed the pieces on the counter and tried to make the edges match.

"Now, let's see," she said, concentrating on the road and the lakes to try and make sure that they were set up properly. When she was satisfied she looked up at Frank.

"Hold this here, will ya," she said. Frank put his hand on the map so that it wouldn't move. She took the end of the tape and pulled out a long piece. She cut it and then grabbed the cut end with her free hand. She looked at the map and judged it for a moment. Then she put one end of the tape at the edge of the two pieces and carefully began allowing the tape to fall where the two pieces came together. Frank moved his hand as she came to it. When she reached the end she ran her hand back down along the end of the tape to flatten it and make sure her job was done correctly. "Five dollars please," she said. Frank pulled out his wallet and gave her a five dollar bill.

"Thanks," said Frank, taking up the map and moving back over to the desk. Once back, Frank began matching the deed numbers again on the piece of paper with those on the map. It was a good photocopy. The numbers were very clear. As he found each piece of land he traced the border with his pen. He placed a check mark beside it on the piece of paper to indicate that it had been found. At first, the pieces of land that Mrs. Ashe owned were scattered all over the northeast part of the county. It didn't seem like anything a provincial park could be made out of. Frank continued. As he went through number after number, the pieces of land began to join one another. First, there were two large blocks. Then there were three with some scattered pieces. Finally, as the numbers on the page became fewer and fewer, Frank saw that, indeed, the series of small pieces of property made up one huge piece of property.

"Son of a bitch," said Frank out loud. He looked to see if the woman had heard him. She hadn't. Frank judged the size of the piece of land with that of the provincial park beside it. They were almost identical.

"Incredible," he thought. He noticed that there was one small piece of land near the southern part of the large block that wasn't part of Mrs. Ashes'. It was on a small lake and it jutted into the larger block. Frank took down the number of the deed and went back to the counter.

"Excuse me, again?" said Frank. She looked up and again slowly got out of her chair. Frank turned away this time. He didn't want her to see him staring. She walked over to the counter.

"What now, dear?" she said with a smile.

"Could you give me the name of the person who owns deed AC 75623?"

"Hold on," she said and took a piece of paper and a pencil out from below the counter.

"What was that number again?" she said.

"Deed AC 75623"

She wrote it down. "Hold on." She walked into the back room where she had put the large book. Frank waited. It didn't take her long and she came back.

"Here," she said handing him a piece of paper. "I wrote down the name for you. If you want a copy of the deed, you'll have to pay five dollars again." She rolled her eyes as if to say "can you believe that".

"Thanks," said Frank and went back to the table. He sat down. He looked at the piece of paper. The name of the person who owned the land was Jon Maitland.

"Holy shit," said Frank. This time the woman did look up.

"Everything all right?" she asked him.

"Yeah, sorry," said Frank. But it wasn't all right. He was shaken. That small finger of land that poked its head up into the vast expanse of land owned by Mrs. Ashe was the same place that he and Willie had been at eight days ago. Frank put his head down on the table. He knew what he had to do next. He turned the piece of paper over and wrote down the name Mrs. Yvonne Ashe. He crossed out the 'Mrs.' and the 'vonne' of Yvonne. Five letters remained. "Y Ashe". He looked at the letters and wrote them down together. Y-A-S-H-E. There it was. It had all come together like the pieces of a puzzle that wasn't supposed to be put back together. How had he come to this point? It didn't seem reasonable or possible. But it had. For some reason there had been an instinct that told him to go on. Every time someone dismissed the name or the idea or the man himself, Frank had felt more and more compelled to move forward. Now he stared at the name Y Ashe. Those letters were spelling out his own fate. He looked at them for a long time, unwilling to take the final step. After what seemed like forever, Frank finally took up his pen again and wrote it.

H-A-Y-E-S.

Chapter 10

Talent for directions was unique, and Frank actually prided himself on his. He liked to tell people that he only had to go to a place once. That was all it took. Then, from that point on, he would be able to find his way back. It didn't matter if the next trip to that location was a week later or a year later, he could get there again. He had a good memory for street names and little details about an area that allowed him to get his bearings quickly. Even if he hadn't gone to a place before, he often would have an intuition about whether to turn left or right at a certain spot. He would play a game with Willie on occasion, when she wasn't in a hurry to get somewhere or when she hadn't had enough of his ramblings on that particular day. If they were going to a new place, one that she knew but he did not, he would ask her to give little details to him, the name of the person, the area of town and the street name. Then he would try and find the place before Willie lost her patience. He was usually able to do it. Willie would always be amazed by it ,although she would try to hide it so as not to arouse his self-congratulatory side, which even he knew could be unbearable.

Trying to find his way to Jonathan's cottage was coming quite easily. The highway was not difficult to find from town.

The long drive north from Huntsville gave him time to remember the road off the highway, the one he now drove down. He remembered that there were a series of turns he would have to make. The last was a right that took him into the driveway that had been hacked out of the woods. He was unsure about that particular turn. The overgrowth of brush caused it to be well hidden from the road. Jonathan was the only person who ever went to the cabin. Since he wasn't there very often, he spent little time or money fixing the road. Besides, he had an off-road truck. It had cost Jonathan a great deal of money and Frank thought it was crazy for someone as tied to the city as Jonathan to have a car like that. But, it was useful getting up that drive. Frank and Willie had had a lot of difficulty in Willie's car. They heard the bottom of the car hit the rocks in the road more than once. Frank wanted to leave the car at the side of the road and walk there. Willie thought that was ridiculous and she drove on, pushing the car up the steep hills to the small parking area at the top.

The first turn that Frank had to take came up on him suddenly and by the time he realized it was the one he should take, he was nearly past it. He steered the car into the gap in the trees, swerved and heard some stones from the road ping into the woods. The quick turn also sent his knapsack flying from the front seat onto the floor. It had not been zipped shut, and almost all the contents fell out onto the floor of the car. Frank looked down to see if everything was ok. It seemed to be. He looked into the rearview mirror at the gap in the forest where the roads met. It became smaller and smaller behind him. There was a long line of trees on either side of the road making a green and brown fence that draped over the road like a canopy. Frank looked at the forest that passed by the car. He tried to look past the first line of trees and see into the forest itself. It was impossible. No light penetrated the tall pines, spruce, and birch trees. They seemed to stretch up to the sun, trying to take from it the light that fed them. Under these hungry beasts were those that had lost the battle to survive in this wilderness. The old trees that had lived their lives and were now forced down by the younger, hungry growth. Smaller trees had fallen because they had been left behind. They had tried to reach above their brothers but they could not. The place that fate chose for them to stand had made it impossible. They lay rotting beside the old, defeated. There were also the new trees, those only a few years old. They were rubbery like all the world's young and life, for now, was easy. They needed little space, and the occasional light that passed through the greedy outstretched hands of their older, larger siblings was enough to feed them. Soon though, they would grow to the point where some would move on to stand among the largest and strongest of those in the forest. The others would be forced out and down. Then, in the end, they would lie broken, lost and dead.

Willie had given Frank a long list of the things that he should buy for his time at Jonathan's. She didn't like that he was going to the cottage without calling Jonathan. But she was certain that Frank wouldn't see anyone there. Jonathan had told her that he would be on Georgian Bay. In any event, it was a weekday and Jonathan would be at work. Willie especially didn't like the fact that Frank would be going into the woods, even only as far as Jonathan's. She had struggled for a long time with her feelings about him setting off alone. The information she could provide would be of little help. Reluctantly, she gave him a list of things to purchase. Frank had gone into a camping store in Huntsville and bought everything. There was a sleeping bag, a ground sheet, and a small tent. He bought candles and a powerful flashlight with extra batteries. He also bought matches and a waterproof case to put them in. The jacket and knapsack he bought were also waterproof. He bought food, some in pouches that was freeze-dried. Willie was sure that he would find coffee and other things at the cabin.

She also gave him a one-page sheet of survival techniques to use in case he became lost. He had looked at them in the store while his purchases were being bagged. It had information about surviving hypothermia and being stranded without anything to keep you warm. It gave ways to make tracks in the woods to find your way back to where you had come from. It even gave advice on how to defend against a bear attack. For some reason, her information seemed to be too extreme and a little unnecessary.

The next turn was easier to spot and Frank took it a little more gently. Now he had to keep an eye out for the drive into Jonathan's cabin. He slowed the car down and checked the right side of the road. He wondered if the little car would make it up the driveway to the parking area. Frank slowed to a stop at a small gap in the trees. He took a deep breath and turned into the trees. He was immersed in the green of the trees. They stood tall beside the car and their branches, like arms, reached over the car as though they were children making a game of creating a tunnel.

Frank switched off the car and put his supplies into the knapsack. He placed it on the ground and then rolled up the window. Mosquitoes buzzed around him. He slapped one on his arm. He closed the car door and dug into the outer pocket of his knapsack for the insect repellent. He slapped away another mosquito on his hand and one on his neck. He grabbed the repellent and started to spray the exposed parts of his body. The mosquitoes seemed to be all over him. He pulled out a hat he had bought in town, a light green fishing hat with a brim that went all the way around. It was canvas and it was stiff. He put it on his head.

He saw a dozen mosquitoes on his jeans, down by his ankles. They were trying to draw blood through the denim. He took up the repellent again and sprayed his clothing. Satisfied that the bugs were gone for the time being, Frank put the spray back in the pocket of his knapsack, put his knapsack over his shoulders, adjusted the straps and then walked into the wilderness along the trail that led to the lake.

By the time Frank reached the cabin, the sun was almost down. Willie had been right, no one was there and no one had been there that weekend. It had been a long day for him. He had sent Willie home, found the courthouse and the information he needed. He had gone to the camping store and bought what he needed, drove to Jonathan's and then walked to the cabin.

He stood on the deck in front of the cabin and looked out onto the dock, the water and the woods on the other side of the lake. Somehow he had hoped that when he got there Hayes would be waiting for him, knowing that he was coming. But no one was there.

Frank put his bag down and walked over to the stairs that led to the dock. He reached under the top rung, trying to find the nail the key hung on. He wiggled the key off the nail, and walked to the door. The padlock on the door was rusty and the key felt as though it might break, but in the end the lock gave way easily. He walked in, took the knapsack from his back and put it on the old couch with the orange and brown polyester covering. The cupboard contained coffee, tea, hot chocolate, powdered cream, fruit drink mix, sugar, salt and pepper, a bag of marshmallows, an unopened jar of smooth peanut butter, some freeze-dried food packets, a box of crackers, some cans of soup and stew and packets of soup, cans of vegetables and three unopened bags of spaghetti. Frank brought his knapsack over. He added three tins of tuna, a heavy loaf of bread, a box of pancake mix, a bottle of syrup, a package of juice boxes, a bag of apples, a carton of eggs, a jar of spaghetti sauce, another bag of spaghetti to add to those already there, and a bottle of Thai rum that he had kept since he had gone to Southeast Asia ten years ago. The rum was the colour of strong tea. The label had Thai writing on it. The only word in arabic script was RUM in bold letters. Frank pulled the covering off and then pulled the cork out. He smelled the rum inside and it gave him a shiver. He remembered drinking a bottle of it in northwestern

Thailand with a group of Canadians from Edmonton. They had had a fun-filled night of drinking and telling old hockey stories. They had drawn a crowd of Germans and Australians who wanted to join in the fun. They began a makeshift game of hockey with an old rubber ball and some brooms used to clean the huts that they were all staying in. The owner finally threatened to call the police. The hangover he had the following day was the worst one he could remember before or since. His head had pounded for nearly three days. Frank had brought a couple of bottles back home, and hadn't thought about them until this trip. He pulled a glass out of the cupboard and poured himself a large amount. He took a sip and let the warm liquid rush down into his belly. Warm memories flowed through his head. Looking at the glass for a moment, he pondered the molasses-coloured liquid. He put the glass down and reached under the counter to lift the propane tank and see how much was there. It was heavy.

The cabin was getting dark. Frank searched for matches by the fireplace. He found them and lit one. On the fireplace mantle he found an oil lamp and lit the wick. A warm glow filled the cabin. It seemed larger in the lamp light. Frank thought about the early settlers who came north. How they had cabins no larger than this to live in year round. Frank saw another lamp on the other side of the cabin, and lit it as well. He picked it up, and walked into the back room where a series of bunk beds were situated. The room could sleep eight people, each in their own bed.

Frank walked back out into the kitchen and picked up his glass of rum. The sun set behind the cabin and the light it gave off turned the green trees into a bright orange wall that reflected on the water. Frank walked down to the dock where he and Willie had sat that morning to watch the sunrise. He sipped the rum and closed his eyes. He listened for a splash in the water.

The next morning, Frank woke up late. He had hoped to be up in time for the sunrise but he hadn't brought an alarm clock to wake him. When he did get up, the sun was already shining brightly over the small lake. He lit the propane stove to make some coffee. He had a bit of a headache. The bottle of rum sat on the counter, one fifth of it gone. He had drunk it in the quiet of the previous night.

Having made coffee and eggs, he cut a piece of bread and went out onto the deck in front of the cabin. The sun had been up long enough to warm the old cracked wood. He moved his bare feet gingerly on the dry surface, sat down on the stairs and put his coffee down beside him. He took up his fork and began eating, looking over the lake. He saw the V in the trees through which the sun had come up that day. It was at the widest part of the lake, where Willie had swum that day. It was perhaps two hundred yards to the other side. He followed the tree line to the right, toward where the man had stood. The shoreline came closer and closer to the cabin as it came across, so that the lake seemed more like a river. The shoreline was perhaps one hundred feet away. He decided he would enter into the woods at that point.

Frank finished his meal, picked up his coffee and took short sips. He could barely hold the hot tin cup. It reminded him of that morning with Willie. He missed her. He took another sip and wondered what he would do. It was well passed 9 a.m. and every minute he stayed on the dock meant a shorter distance he would travel that day. That made him think for a moment. How far could he get? Where would he go? Was he going to be able to find his way back? Was it all worth it? That last question was the easiest to answer. He had asked it of himself so many times. Since the first day that the name Hayes found its way to his ears, it had been pushing him. The man himself, Frank couldn't help but think, was forcing, pushing him to follow his instincts and not his head. Frank stood up with a sudden movement. He couldn't wait any longer.

He walked back into the cabin and put the plate into a large tub. He washed the plate and frying pan. He finished his coffee in one long gulp. He checked the contents of his knap-sack. It contained the sleeping bag, the ground sheet and the small tent. There was also a waterproof case for the matches. Frank took out the insect repellent and gave himself a heavy dose all over. He also packed a flashlight, and from Jonathan's toolbox he packed a knife and small hatchet.

He remembered Willie saying that it would get cold at night. Willie's voice had been mechanical, as though she had been reciting her times table. But the idea sent a shiver down Frank's spine. What if he got lost? He and Willie had made a deal that he would drive into town by Sunday and call her no matter what. That gave him a week. If he didn't call her, she would assume that something was wrong. But if he were lost, what could she do?

Frank walked down to the short long-hut where the canoes were kept. He swung open the heavy wooden door and pulled the shorter canoe, the green one, forward. Turning it over, he picked it up and carried it to the water. He went back, picked up a paddle, and then closed the door, grabbing his knapsack. He looked back for a moment, almost saying goodbye to some-one. He pushed the canoe into the water and stepped in. He took up the paddle, pushed off from the rocks, and headed to the area where he had first seen the man.

It was a short distance across but it took some time. Frank didn't know how to handle a canoe and he couldn't help but make a zigzag pattern across the small channel until he finally reached the other side. He pulled himself close to the shore and then carefully raised himself to the point where he could put one foot onto the land. He leaned his weight on his foot and pulled himself out of the canoe. He placed his knapsack onto the shore. He then rolled the canoe over and put the paddle under it. He slipped his knapsack over his shoulders. As though he were about to submerge himself into the lake, he took a deep breath and then plunged into the woods.

The glow from the firelight was all he had to see by, but it was enough to paint everything orange. Frank took the cloth from his face and felt the deep scratch across his forehead. It was a gouge that had only stopped bleeding after hours of applied pressure. Frank sat on the floor in front of the fire. He felt as if he were back in the woods looking at a camp fire. His first trip out had been a disaster, ending hours ago, when after a day and a half of twisting and turning his way through the dense forest, he came out at the far end of Jonathan's lake. He had a deep cut on his forehead that bled into his eyes and a long bruise on his shin where he had fallen down an unseen ravine.

Time in the forest could not be measured conventionally. It was rather a series of ups and downs, dense brush and clearings, streams and ponds. He had spent the night sitting beside a smouldering fire, trying to keep it burning without constant attention. He didn't even get his tent set up and instead sat with his sleeping bag over his shoulders staring at the smoking mess. Walking through the dense brush had been difficult. At times he could barely move. The trees and their branches seemed to enclose him, grabbing at his arms and his legs, holding him. It was impossible to go forward. If Hayes was out there, he had savage, insane followers protecting him. Hayes, thought Frank, it is just a name after all. That was all it could be. How could he find him?

Frank poked the dark orange embers. They crackled as sparks rose up the chimney. He brought the bottle of rum to his lips. It was more than half empty now. He had used some of it to disinfect his wound. The sting of the alcohol was so intense that Frank had nearly passed out. It continued to bleed and he had to make something to eat using only one hand, as the other held the bandage.

He ate well that night and got drunk. The next day he would face whatever there was left for him. He wondered if there was anything at all. Perhaps not. Carl had told him that everything would be all right. Maybe it was time to just realize what he was, one of Stone's boys. Nothing but a mouthpiece. And why not? It gave him what he wanted didn't it? He had Willie, and he always would have. Didn't he have his photo over his column? Shit, so many people tried so hard to get where he was, didn't it mean something? Perhaps he had been travelling down the right stream the whole time. Maybe this whole trip into the woods was simply his reaction to the fact that it was coming all too easily for him.

When the cut stopped bleeding, he used both hands to roast some marshmallows. He watched them turn brown, and placed them in his mouth, letting their warmth slide down his throat.

Frank's forehead throbbed and his leg was so bruised that it made him limp. He unlocked the car door and threw the knapsack into the passenger seat. He lowered himself slowly into the driver's seat, pulled the door closed and started up the engine. The rattle that had begun during the bumpy drive up to the cabin was more pronounced now. This will cost me, he thought. He let the car run for a bit, giving it a chance to ready itself for the hard drive down the hill. There would be more bumps and Frank just hoped that everything would stay attached until he returned the car to the rental agency.

He shifted the gear into reverse and backed the car out from between the two trees. Clear of them, he started down the slope toward the road and back to Huntsville. The first hill was smooth. The car didn't rock at all through the ruts in the road. He negotiated the turns and then headed through the next grade. He couldn't help but feel like a rally car driver. He sped up and felt a rare exhilaration. At the bottom of the hill he had to turn sharply and he did it with a kind of precision that he didn't know he had. He pushed the accelerator further and the car was sped through the trees, missing them by inches. He hit the next slope with such speed that he couldn't help but feel the car had left the ground. It came down with a thunderous clap of steel and rock hammering together. The sound made Frank push the car even harder. The last few turns were the tightest, and he felt the back end fly out. Then he saw a hole in the forest. A clear patch of sunlight lay ahead where the road was. The opening rushed at him, and in one great surge he was free and onto the sunny road. He slammed the brakes, clutching the steering wheel, his knuckles white. He looked behind and saw nothing but a cloud of dust. He was sweating and the cut on his forehead throbbed so quickly that it felt like one continuous pain.

He thought for a moment about what he had just done. He could have easily killed himself. The acceleration waned for a moment. What the hell had he been thinking? He could've been there for days. Willie would have eventually sent someone, but he surely would be dead by then. He thought about all of Willie's cautions. He had followed them all. Everything she told him to keep him safe. Something about being in that car made him forget all of that. It had become a kind of armour.

Driving back, Frank was taken with the beauty around him. The greens, the blues, and the browns all blended together to make a colour that defied definition. Off in the distance, seeming more like giants watching over everything than like the school children he had pictured earlier, were the electrical towers. How could anyone escape those structures? Frank thought about the days without electricity, gasoline and jet fuel. What a world it must have been.

The long row of electrical poles stood along the road. They carried things that people could no longer live without. In the weakness of the new age, people needed electricity, telephones and cable TV. As Frank drove down the road he noticed all those lines heading south. His head was upturned, staring at the lines and the blue sky beyond. He didn't see the sharp curve until he was almost off the road. He was going too fast. The car went off the side of the road. He hit the brake and the back end swung out. The car was in a skid and Frank steered hard to avoid one of the electrical poles. He came to a stop in the middle of the road, facing the pole he was just romancing. He took a deep breath. The car was still running and Frank realized that both his feet were pushed down hard on the brake. Putting the car in park, he released one foot. The road was empty. He took another deep breath and looked over at the pole again. There was something strange about it, but he couldn't put his finger on it. It seemed just like an old electrical pole. What was unusual? He followed the pole from the ground to the top. It was exactly like the other ones. Frank looked to his right to see the next one in line. But there was none. He looked to his left. Again, nothing. He looked at the top of the pole, where the wires went. One went over the car and was attached to the poles on the south side of the road. The other wire disappeared into the forest.

Frank's heart nearly burst.

Chapter 11

Frank rushed through the trees, the branches slapping his face, his arms, body and legs. The knapsack bounced on his back. He followed the line of wooden poles. As he went further into the trees, the next pole became harder for him to see. He would stop and follow the electrical line until he could see the next marker. It was a path he was sure would lead to Hayes.

Sitting in the car, Frank had felt a moment of euphoria that he had never known before. His face went red and the sheer pounding in his chest drove him to run into the forest. The next pole was in sight. He raced toward it. He had parked the car far enough off the road so that it could be seen but not accidentally run into, although he imagined few people actually drove down that road. The line of poles was on the land that Hayes owned, Frank knew that. But where did they lead? How far could it be? Frank thought about what was in his bag. He had taken everything from Jonathan's so as not to leave any trace that he had been there. All the food and the flashlight and the rum. He had his tent and his sleeping bag. He would be fine if he had to stay in the woods overnight.

The next pole was up a steep embankment. The ground was loose but he pumped his legs in football drill fashion to get to the top. The last few feet were straight up and Frank had to actually grab an old stump and pull himself up. He swung his legs onto the ground and pulled himself up until he lay on his side on the top of the ridge. Through the dense forest he could see the sunshine. He stood up and brushed off the leaves and twigs that were on him. He looked back and saw the slope he had just climbed. He was glad he didn't know how steep or how high it had been. Frank walked toward the sun. There seemed to be nothing past the trees. It looked as though it was the end of the world. He reached the edge and looked out onto a vast valley. He stood on the edge of a cliff that dropped at least two hundred feet into the forest. He looked at the electrical pole he'd followed up to this ridge. The wires led to it, but they did not lead from it. Instead they dropped down and hung rotting. Frank walked over to the pole and looked at the wires. By the clean break Frank assumed that they had been cut. This was where the power ended.

Frank looked out onto the Canadian Shield. The green went for miles, broken only by the occasional outcrop of rock and the blue of the small lakes. It was like some northern green sea, its waves rolling toward rocky shores of granite. He felt small, like a fishing boat away from its harbour, travelling up and down the great walls of water. He looked to the sky to gain a navigation point. The sun was setting in front of him, slowly dropping below the waves.

Frank wiped the sweat from his forehead. He touched his cut, and it stung. He slipped the knapsack off his back and leaned it against the old electrical pole, then took off his long shirt and stood bare-chested. The wind caught the beads of sweat on his arms and neck; it gave him goosebumps. He reached into the knapsack, took out a t-shirt and put it on. He had been pushing through the forest for nearly six hours. The evidence was clear now. Hayes must have had these lines put up. He owned the land. He would have had to pay for the lines and the electricity. Sloan paid the rate. But the lines were cut some time ago. Did Hayes live for a while on this cliff? It had a great view. You could see for a hundred miles into the valley. Perhaps Hayes knew that he could be found through those lines. That is how they get you. They hook you up on those lines and offer you more and more until you can't refuse. Then, once you're online, they have you. The world can find you without so much as a second thought. He kicked a small rock by the side of the cliff and watched it fall into the forest below. The trees reached up the side of the rock wall. From this angle they looked like green pins stuck into a huge map. There were dead trees as well, standing grey and branchless. He saw one below him. It seemed lifeless and still beside the branches of the evergreens. The dead tree had two branches left that were short and jutted out of either side of the top. He kicked another stone and watched it fall to the bottom of the cliff. It disappeared into the forest below. Frank couldn't hear it land.

Frank woke early the next morning and could barely stand. His legs were sore from the long day's hike. He had camped on the top of the cliff. He needed time to figure out how the tent was put together. It had taken him nearly an hour to put the small nylon shelter up and afterwards it didn't seem like much. Now, getting up, he thought about the comfort of the night's sleep. It was wonderful. The night breeze was refreshing, coming through the small zippered windows that he'd allowed to hang open so that he wouldn't suffocate. He stretched, walking around to loosen his legs. He limped slightly, still bothered by the leg with the bruised shin. After a short while he felt fine. The pain was a wonderful thing. Each movement sent a small reminder from a muscle that Frank hadn't exercised in years. Each small jolt told him that he had tendons and joints. It felt great to be in touch with his body, even if it meant suffering.

He made a small fire, ate some bread, and had some tuna from the can. He used a small pot to boil some water and had some coffee without cream or sugar. It wasn't as bad as he thought. He stood up with some difficulty and walked over to the edge of the cliff. He looked again at the great expanse of wilderness. You could easily lose yourself from the rest of the world in the great green abyss. Hayes had done it well. Frank didn't want it to happen to him. How foolish it was to think that people had tamed the world. That was the arrogance of humanity. To think that someone could look out onto a valley like this and feel that it was gentle! Nature still controlled this world regardless of what people thought. He felt that. It was so easy. Sitting in the middle of a city with everything done for you. Every aspect of life catered. It was so easy. Those who grumbled now seemed so ridiculous. People so distracted with themselves that they forgot that just beyond the edge of the concrete that protected them was a world that was wild, hungry, and without remorse. It had no morality. It lived only to survive. Nothing more. Art, culture and money meant nothing. The only currency was strength and will. That was all.

Frank had no reason to think he could survive once his food ran out. He could see from the cliff that there was water, but his provisions were getting low. He had a tin of tuna and nearly a full loaf of bread. He had juice and eggs that were unbroken, even after the trip through the woods. He had a bag of spaghetti and a box of soup mix from Jonathan's. The pouches remained as well. He had some coffee, and what was left of the bottle of rum. It was maybe four days worth, that was it. Then what? He kicked a rock off the cliff again. It flew far out from the cliff. It fell spinning, down toward the dead tree at the bottom of the cliff. It fell without a sound. He looked at the dead grey wood of the tree. The two branches that came from both sides were so short and stubby and straight that they didn't look real. He went down onto his knees and leaned his head to get as close to the tree as he could, as if the extra five feet would make some sort of difference. It wasn't a tree at all. It was another electrical pole. Of course it was. Frank looked further out into the valley. There was another pole nestled between the trees. It was hard to see but it was there.

"You old bastard," he said out loud, smiling. The sound of his voice startled him. He had not spoken for days. He began getting ready to climb down into the valley.

Frank slid his way down the side of the cliff toward the tall old electrical pole. He kept his eye on it the entire time so as not to lose his bearings. The rocks on his hands felt hard and sharp. He would stop periodically and feel them in his hands. They had been warmed by the sun. Their texture was both rough and smooth. He looked at his hands on the rocks. They didn't seem out of place and for a moment he thought of himself as a climber. What was that like, to climb a mountain using your bare hands? To hang from the rocks and ice of a mountain face simply to get to the top? Enormous risk and for what gain? Certainly not fame. He could only think of two climbers. One was Edmund Hillary, the New Zealander who was the first to climb Everest. The other was the Canadian who followed that path thirty years later. What was his name? Frank tried to think. He had seen him interviewed afterwards. But what had happened to him since? No, they didn't climb for glory or riches. There was a different passion that drove them. And now he was closer to knowing that passion than ever before. He touched the rocks again and then gripped them firmly and began to climb down. As he came close to the bottom, he left the sunny brown rocks of the cliff and began to descend into the dark green forest below. Just before he was completely out of the sun's light, he looked out at the tops of the trees, took a deep breath and plunged downward.

When he reached the bottom he had to follow the face of the cliff to the pole. The underbrush was thicker than he had ever seen it and it grabbed at his arms and knapsack. He worked his way through to the old grey pole. He put his hands on it as though he were feeling for a pulse. It was long since dead. He looked up the cliff to where he had stood. It didn't seem as high as it had from the top. Very little light had managed to find its way down to the forest. Somewhere in the darkness, surrounded by large brown trees, was the old grey pole that he hoped, with the help of a long line of others just like it, would lead him to Hayes.

Frank continued for the next two and a half days. At times he lost the trail but then he would backtrack and find it again. He was tired and dirty. The terrain was by no means flat and the trees and undergrowth were unyielding. At night he had better luck, starting fires and setting up the tent, finding ample flat spaces under tall pine trees. The needles under the tent created a comfortable bed and he slept well, waking only on occasion to the sound of rustling leaves and wind. At one point on the second night he heard animal sounds and his heart raced during the scraping and shuffling. In the morning he found scratch marks on the rope that held his knapsack high above the ground and well away from his tent. He was relieved he had remembered Willie's tip.

Near the end of his third day he spotted the blue of a pond through the trees. He marked the pole with an orange marker he'd brought for that purpose and did the same on trees every ten feet until he reached the water's edge. He looked back into the woods and saw the bright, neon tags well into the forest. The lake was small and surrounded by a thick growth of small trees. He followed the shoreline with his eyes, looking for a place where he could get close to the water. He saw none, so he put a marker on the branch of a healthy tree and began making his way around the shore of the lake. About fifty yards from the point where he'd come out of the woods he found a small flat area of rock he could put his back against, and sit for a while. The rock felt cold, as though it never received the warmth of the summer sun. He took off his pack and placed it on the rock. He went to the water and leaned down, putting his face in like an animal. He took a long drink of the cool green water, then wiped his face with his hand. The sun lit an area in the middle of the water. He had been submerged in the forest for hours and he missed the sun on his face. He removed his clothes and threw them on his pack. He stood on the rock naked. He felt a cool breeze and he couldn't help but turn his head to see if anyone was looking. He had never gone skinny dipping like Willie had. The only times he had been naked was indoors, as strange as that seemed now. He crossed his arms and looked down, remembering the warnings to look before diving into water. All he could see was green. Stepping into the water, he shivered. The water was cool against his skin. He moved slowly until he was in at mid-thigh. He took small steps until the cool water touched his penis and he jumped back. He thought about going back. But out in the middle of the lake was the sun, shining brightly. Frank cupped his hands and put them in the water. He splashed the water on his body, gritting his teeth. Then, in one motion, he took a step and dove in. He began to swim, head up, out to the bright area.

By the time he had dried off, it was late in the afternoon. He set up his tent on the flat rock and then lit a fire. He made coffee and ate some bread. He looked out onto the pond as the last of the sun's light dangled along the tops of the trees. The brightest of the stars already hung in the sky. The night began to get cool and he reached for another piece of wood from the large pile that he had collected. He looked for a thick piece. Most of the wood was small and dry, so it burned quickly. I need an ax, he thought. That way he could cut larger pieces from the fallen trees along the shore. He thought about other things he would need. A knife, one that had a thick blade and sturdy handle. A better pair of boots as well. They would have to be waterproof. It hadn't rained but Frank thought about the days of rain in the early spring and knew that they would have to withstand a downpour. He thought about the winter which would be hard and would require a whole new set of provisions. The wood on the fire sent embers into the sky. He followed them up and watched as one by one they burned out and disappeared leaving only the stars and the moon to light the sky.

Frank woke in the tent with the smell of smoke still on him. He had sat for hours the night before staring at the fire. As the night grew cooler, he drew nearer to the flames. How warm the little fire had been. He even had a few marshmallows and a shot of rum to make it a perfect evening. He brought his arm to his nose to smell. How strong the fire smell was. The flannel felt warm against his cold nose. He drew a long breath from his sleeve. It was as if the fire was still going. He propped himself up. There was smoke coming through the screen of the little zippered window. Was the fire still going from the night before? He sat up fully and looked through the window at the fire. It was. There was fresh wood in the fire. Frank scrambled out of his sleeping bag, trying but failing to be quiet. He pulled himself to the zippered entrance and pulled it open. He stuck his head out at the fire.It had been almost dead when he had gone to sleep.

"Good morning," said a voice that sent Frank twisting and turning out of the tent. He got one foot out of the tent and tried to stand before the other was out fully, and he tripped over the lip of the small zippered door and went tumbling toward the fire. A strong hand grabbed him.

"Easy," said the man in a quiet calm tone. Frank looked up at him. The man was old, with a bald head and a short full grey beard. He smiled as he helped Frank to his feet. Frank looked at his eyes. They were a blue that was brilliant and warm. It was an unimaginable blue, meditative and bright. He had seen it before, only once.

"Are you all right?" asked the man, stepping back from Frank to give him a chance to get himself together. He walked around Frank to the fire and took up a pot that Frank had almost knocked over. He reached down by Frank's knapsack and picked up his cup.

"Would you like some coffee?" he asked. The smile was still on his face. His skin was wrinkled and weathered. It was a dark brown colour from the sun. He was Frank's height, maybe an inch taller. That would make him an even six feet. His beard was cut short in a meticulous way. But his eyes were what Frank was staring at. They were magnetic and he was unable to turn away from them. Frank had never seen eyes as calm and as full of warmth. But the colour was also something unique, and it echoed in his mind. Frank reached out and took the coffee cup. The old man smiled and walked over to the side of Frank's tent, where his pack lay on the ground. He kneeled down and pulled out a coffee cup for himself. He walked back to where Frank was standing. He poured himself a cup, and sat by the water's edge with his back to Frank.

The old man took off his boots and put his feet into the pond. Unlike his face, the skin on his feet was white and without wrinkles. Frank took a step toward the old man and stopped. The old man took a drink from his coffee cup. Frank managed another step toward him. He tried to speak but couldn't. He could not think of words or of sounds. He just stood and looked at the old man.

"I'm Ford Hayes," said the old man. He took another drink of coffee. "I haven't had a good cup of coffee for a while," he said, splashing his feet in the water. Frank nearly fainted. His heart was beating so hard that it made his chest hurt. The blood rushed from his face and he felt his skin go cold. He began to see stars and his hands began to shake. He felt like he might fall on his knees. He tried again to get his body to move but he couldn't.

"It'll be another glorious day," said Hayes. Frank sat down where he was and then he found the strength to drink from his cup. He gulped the coffee as though it were cool river water.

Hayes turned back to look at Frank, still smiling.

"I didn't mean to startle you," he said. He turned back to the pond. "What's your name?"

"Frank," managed Frank in a boyish tone.

"Well Frank," said Hayes, "Welcome. You know you've picked a good spot to camp. I like this little pond. It is bigger than a pond, really, but it isn't much of a lake. What are you, Frank? A hunter or a fisherman?"

"I'm a reporter," said Frank, not recognizing the sound of his own voice. He gave the answer almost as a reflex, not really aware that he was doing it. There was a long silence.

"Oh. A little bit of both, then," said Hayes. His voice was calm but commanding. It had a quality that Frank had never heard before. "How did you find your way here?"

"The electrical poles," said Frank

"Ah, yes," said Hayes, bowing his head down as though he had been bettered in some game. "Electrical poles." Hayes sat quietly for a moment.

"Why?" Hayes asked, without elaborating. Frank knew what he was asking.

"Something just pulled me toward you." Frank was sorry he had said it in that way. "I was just following up a good story," he continued trying to make it sound as though it were some professional mission.

"I didn't know there was a good story out here."

Frank thought about that day on the lake with Willie. The strange course of events that followed had led him to this. He was sitting and talking to a man that the world had thought long gone. He had never really thought about what he would say once he finally found Hayes. Meeting Hayes had always been, in the far reaches of his mind, the furthest possibility. Searching for Hayes had been the real goal. That had taken courage. He had left everything behind and went out to find a man that he was sure did not exist. Even if Hayes were still alive, he was sure he would never see him or hear him or talk to him. But here he was.

They sat for a long time. Neither spoke. The coffee in Frank's cup had gone cold but he continued to sip it. For some reason Frank didn't feel uncomfortable about sitting. Hayes sat with his feet in the water the entire time, splashing playfully, murmuring something in a low tone. Frank thought he was singing. Now and again Frank shifted from where his bottom was getting numb and tried to find a more comfortable position. He tried to move slowly, without noise. He didn't understand why he was doing that, he simply felt that it was appropriate. After a while he wondered if Hayes was even aware that he was sitting there with him.

"Would you like to go for a walk?" asked Hayes. He surprised Frank, who suppressed a startled noise in the back of his throat. "Um," was all Frank could say.

"Wonderful." With that, Hayes stood up, picked up his boots and began walking toward the woods. He came next to Frank and stopped.

"Need a hand?" he asked Frank.

"Um."

"Are you sure?" Hayes asked, putting out his hand. Frank felt its strong grip. He pulled Frank to his feet. "You should put your boots on."

The two men stood face to face. Frank looked again into Hayes' eyes.

"Reg Sloan paints the colour of your eyes," said Frank.

Hayes looked at him warmly, "I know." He picked up his pack and began walking into the woods. Frank grabbed his boots out of the tent and pulled them on without tying them up. He took up his knapsack and followed Hayes into the forest.

Frank followed Hayes as he made his way through the dense forest. Hayes walked slowly but without hesitation. Frank admired the way he stepped. It was like a mantra of steps, regular and precise. After what seemed like hours, Frank heard the quiet roar of water hitting rocks. They were nearing a river. The ground began to slope in a steep fashion. Hayes walked on, unencumbered by the steepness of the slope. Frank had to hang on to the trees they passed.

Below them Frank could see the clearing through which the river he had heard earlier ran. At the bottom, by the river bank, Hayes stopped and let Frank catch up. Frank came beside the old man in a last flurry of motion, trying to keep himself from falling down the last bit of the slope.

"My place is across the river," said Hayes, pointing to a small opening in the trees across the river. Frank looked at the water rushing by them. It was fast-flowing, with blasts of white water rising up over hidden rocks. Hayes moved into the water, holding his boots above his waist. Frank realized that the river would reach to his waist at least. He thought about taking off his boots. What lay at the bottom of a river like this? Keeping them on, Frank followed Hayes into the water. He immediately felt the pressure of the water trying to push him along with it on its journey toward some final meeting of waters. He stood for a moment, knee-deep in the river, thinking about the journey of such a river.

He moved further and saw Hayes ahead of him in water past his waist and near his armpits. His motion was slow but steady. He knew what he was doing. Frank followed. The water was soon at his waist. The push was incredible. It made Frank think of a concert he'd been to. He was near the front of the stage. The motion of the crowd was against him, trying desperately to get to the stage. People were everywhere around him, pushing ahead. He remembered trying to stand firm against the crowd. It seemed impossible. The motion of the river was like that but even more uncontrollable and frightening. It took all of his strength to resist it.

Hayes reached the other side and looked back at Frank as he struggled through the water. Frank thrust his legs forward. They felt as though they were in cement. He stopped after each step to regain his strength for the next. As he came closer to the shore, the water didn't seem to get any shallower. Hayes stood on the bank of the far side smiling. Frank reached out with his legs as he walked, exploring the bottom of the river. He kicked his right foot and then his left foot forward and was up to his shoulders in water. He felt the rush around his ears. It pushed on his chest and made it hard to breathe. For a moment Frank panicked. The pack on his shoulders had filled with water and was weighing him down further. Frank began to struggle. Just then, the old man reached down and grabbed Frank's arm. He felt himself lifted out of the river and onto the bank.

Standing by Hayes, Frank tried to look unmoved by what had happened. Hayes smiled, turned, and went into the narrow gap in the tall trees by the side of the river. Frank followed. Frank squinted to see while his eyes adjusted. He looked behind him in an uncontrollable reflex to check for onlookers. Hayes sat by a small stove-like structure made from river stones, his pack beside him. There was an iron grill on it that looked ancient. He lit a fire.

Frank felt he had to say something.

"Is this home for you?" he said, realizing too late that he was trying to sound folksy. Hayes chuckled, but did not respond. Frank looked around at the rest of the small clearing. There was a small hut made from logs at the far end. It wasn't very large, probably ten feet by ten feet. The roof itself was another ten feet high at the peak. It had one glass window in a small door that was only six feet high. A long line ran from one tree to another and there were a couple of pieces of clothing hanging to dry. Near that was a pile of wood that was large and ready for winter. A bench made of long thin branches wrapped together sat by the river. That was all. Maybe there was more inside the cabin, thought Frank. Hayes was blowing on the ashes of an old fire, trying to catch small pieces of split wood. His blue eyes were charged with mission as he breathed until his face was red. Then, a spark, and a flame rose from the little group of ashes and wood. Hayes laughed with a sort of joy when this happened, as if it were the first time he had ever done it.

"We'll have some lunch in a minute," said Hayes. He walked past Frank and disappeared into the small cabin. Frank wondered about the time. Was it lunchtime? Had they been sitting by his tent since breakfast? Frank took his soaked backpack off and put it down by the fire. Hayes re-emerged from the cabin with some bread, a pan, a large bottle of yellow liquid that looked like cooking oil and a long pole that looked like a fishing rod. Frank understood the fishing rod and the pan, but the bread and the oil Hayes could only get in town. He assumed Hayes had been going into one of the nearby towns for provisions.

"I hope you like fish," said Hayes, putting down the pan and the bread by the fire. He walked out to the river and knelt down by the water. He placed his hand in the water. He reached for a small can submerged halfway and pulled it out. He opened the lid and reached inside. Hayes pulled out a small, green, moving blob. It was a small frog. Hayes stood smiling at it as though the frog was going to smile back. Hayes replaced the lid and put the can back. He reached for the fishing pole and brought the hook to the frog and placed it gently into the roof of the frog's mouth. Frank winced. Hayes let some line out from the fishing rod and threw the frog and hook into a quiet pool of dark green water downriver.

Frank felt more calm now, watching the water run past them. He was amazed at the amount of noise that came from the river. It was a highway. Hayes was serene and calm.

"Why..." began Frank, but suddenly Hayes jerked the rod back toward him and it bent sharply. Hayes began to crank the old rod, bringing the line and the fish toward them. Frank couldn't help but feel excited.

"Catch him as I pull him up," said Hayes. With a quick jerk the fish was on the shore dancing around under Frank. It bounced against his legs, and Frank gave a small jump. Hayes leaned down and trapped the fish against the rock of the shore. He put the pole down and took the fish up in both hands. He removed the hook from its mouth. The frog was still there, uneaten. Hayes took the frog off the hook and threw it into the area where he had hooked the fish.

"Oh, that's a big one," said Hayes, smiling at Frank. Hayes bent down and took a knife from his pocket. He beat the fish with a rock and then pulled the blade of the knife out. He cleaned the fish, throwing unusable parts back into the river. It took him seconds to finish the job. He put the blade back into the knife handle and returned the knife to his pocket.

Hayes walked back into the forest clearing toward the stove. The fire was burning brightly now. He took some wood and placed it into the fire. He put the fish fillets down on the rock of the stove. He poured some oil into the pan, and then put the pan on the fire. After a few seconds, he then put the fish into the pan. It began to sizzle immediately. The fire mingled with the cooking fish was a smell Frank had never experienced before.

Hayes cut a piece of bread for each of them and put a piece of the fish on each. He gave one piece to Frank and took the other piece. He closed his eyes, his lips moving but not chewing. He opened his eyes again and motioned for Frank to eat. The fish was soft, with a mild taste, and was very refreshing.

Hayes walked over to the bench by the river. Frank followed. They sat and watched the river jumping and arguing in front of them. Frank took another bite and looked at Hayes. He had almost finished his fish. His mouth was full and there were crumbs of bread on his beard.

"Why did you come here? I mean, what were you looking for here?" asked Frank. Hayes' smile brightened. His eyes narrowed and focused on the river in front of them.

"I can only answer that," said the old man, "by asking you the same question. Why are you here?"

"I came to find you." Frank wasn't sure if he was telling him or asking him.

"That seems foolish," said Hayes. Frank was stung. His

heart pounded, and he could feel the cold water on his body turn to hot sweat. He wanted to tell Hayes about that day on the dock of Jonathan's cottage. No, he didn't want to tell him, he felt he had to tell him. Tell him about the man on the far side of the lake, who disappeared into the trees. He wanted to discuss the dinner he had with Trish and Richard and mention that Willie was a relative of his. He wanted to tell him about how Carl reacted when he saw the name Cecil Rutherford Hayes on the computer screen. He wanted to tell him about Carlisle and Stone. About Stone's history stories. How they had basically threatened him. No, more than threatened, how they had made him feel, well, meaningless, not worth being threatened. A child who needed to be shown his place. He wanted to tell him about Gillis and the story Gillis had heard from Stone's first wife. About the Jewish boy standing in front of the cheering crowd of the sons of the wealthy. But how could he? How could he tell him all these things and explain how these things happened one by one?

Frank felt a rush that he could not explain. Something deep inside him as dark as the forest and as remote as their camp. Foolish? How could it be foolish? It had pushed him, tormented and questioned him. It made him look inside himself and wonder what his life was and what he thought it might lead to. It compelled him to rush into the forest, leaving comfort and safety and career and all desires that seemed normal and plunge into the danger and darkness of the forest. Trying to find this ghost who had haunted these woods, falsely, for thirty years. How could Frank tell these things to this man, who sat looking at the river with blue eyes that were so remarkable? Sloan had spent his entire life contemplating and then expressing that blue. Now, Frank's journey was called foolish.

"It was a good story," said Frank, trying to sound distant from the thoughts that raged in his head.

Hayes looked at Frank briefly then turned back to the river. "That's a very professional answer." Hayes was silent, then began to murmur to himself. It was like a song that he had in his head that he couldn't help but hum as he sat quietly. Thoughts were moving across the wires of Frank's head like lightning across the plains, hitting at memories and ideas with jolts that made his eyelids blink and his body shake.

Frank always had questions. That was his trademark. If a person gave him five minutes or an hour, Frank could fill it with questions, asking and scribbling in his notepad while his tape recorder ran. Even if he had the information he needed, he never stopped asking questions until the subject left or demanded that he stop. But here he was without questions, yet he wanted so many answers. Frank turned to the river. The water was hypnotic as it moved in front of him. It moved past him without care.

Maybe he had been wrong. Perhaps he was right in finding this man by the river, but as with many of the stories he had covered, beyond the facts, beyond the elements that made the story telling, there was nothing. It was just a story. Suddenly, Frank felt sorry for Hayes. This poor old hermit, living among the trees, deep in a forest.

Hayes turned to Frank. "I saw that you had a bottle of something in that haversack of yours." His smile went large again. Frank stared at the brilliant colour of his eyes. Frank stood up and went to his pack by the fire. Small orange, yellow and red flames still burned. Hayes must keep this fire going, thought Frank. He went through his bag and found the bottle of rum. It was still half full. Hayes must have gone through Frank's bag when Frank was still asleep. Frank wondered what he might have been looking for.

"Here you are," said Frank, taking the cap off and handing the bottle to Hayes. Hayes held the bottle under his nose, inhaling deeply. It was as though the smell took him somewhere. Perhaps he could attach himself to the vapours that rose from the bottle into the wind and off across the sky to places that were only memories now. Hayes put the bottle to his lips and drank. He passed the bottle to Frank. The sweet rum was barely felt in Frank's throat as it warmed him. Frank offered the bottle back to Hayes but the old man waved it off.

"That was enough for me," he said, and turned back to the river. Frank took another drink and put the cap back on the bottle. He placed the bottle between them on the bench.

"Are you a writer?" asked Hayes in his quiet, firm voice. "Or are you a radio or television person?"

"I write," said Frank, noticing for the first time the tears and rips in Hayes' clothing.

"What do you write?"

"I write about Toronto."

"Is that your passion?"

"I, I guess it is."

"Good. Who is your publisher?"

"John Carlisle," said Frank. Hayes laughed.

"So, you work for Harold Stone, do you?" said Hayes. Frank was amazed. How did he know that? Did he know Stone that well? Stone hadn't bought the paper until six years ago. Did Sloan tell him? He must have.

"Not really, but, yes, I suppose I do," said Frank. He turned to look at the river. The sun was going down and the green of the trees that reached out over the water was turning shades of purple and orange. The water seemed to calm as the evening came. The sky was clear.

"I see," said Hayes.

"How long has Sloan been trustee of your land?" asked Frank.

"Since the day I came here," said Hayes. "I set up the lands after I purchased them, to be in his trust until the day that Mrs. Yvonne Ashe died. I take it you know who she is. A joke of Sloan's. I also have him meet me twice a year at a given point on the boundary of the land with a specific amount of provisions. I regret that idea now because I've had to keep track of the years and months and days so as to meet him. I tried to stop that, but Reg liked our meetings."

Reg Sloan had kept this secret for so long. Frank knew powerful people in important positions who considered themselves as having substance and integrity who couldn't keep their mouths shut for an hour. Sloan had done it while they searched for and pronounced Hayes dead, for the second time. It was the first time Frank realized the true power that love could hold over someone. He continued with his questions.

"Is this where you came the first time you left?" Frank didn't want to say "disappeared." But he couldn't help himself now. He needed to know.

"No," said Hayes. Frank could sense that Hayes was reluctant to reveal where he had been and for the first time the smile on Hayes's face left as he lost himself in the memory of that first time away.

"Where did you go?" asked Frank. Hayes smiled again.

"That's unimportant." The smile returned to Hayes' face.

"Did you tell your family where you went?" asked Frank.

"No." There was silence except for the river.

"Is it lonely here?" asked Frank. Hayes' lips curled as he watched the river. Frank also watched the flowing greenish brown water. He looked beyond it to the trees and followed the slope of the land into the forest. Frank looked at the tall trees that were like soldiers standing for inspection. He put his hand on the bench and felt the smooth thin branches. They had become worn over the years of Hayes sitting and looking at the river. Frank saw Hayes as a quiet gentle man. He wondered if that was in spite of or because of the years that he had spent living in this forest by the water flowing in front of them.

Then, in a low voice, Hayes spoke. Frank looked up.

"Do you know where this river starts?" he asked Frank.

"No."

"Neither do I," said Hayes. "Do you know where it ends?"

"No."

"Neither do I. But I do know that where it begins and where it ends aren't important. What is important is that it flows. It doesn't care whether I am here or whether I am away. It flows. In it there is life and death but no remorse. There is beauty and respect but no hatred or greed. It is strong and ever-lasting but it doesn't know how to be arrogant. At the same time, it is beginning and ending. Isn't that incredible. Every second, it is living all of its life. While it does that, it doesn't worry about me or anything or anybody else that takes from it. It gives me comfort if I wish to take it, but it doesn't ask me for any.

"Listen to it. Close your eyes." Hayes motioned to Frank. "What do you hear? Water, water on rocks, a voice, a thousand voices or perhaps more. The sound of the river means many things, it tells many stories and every one of those stories are mine and yours."

Frank realized that Hayes wasn't really speaking to him. Instead, he was speaking some long remembered mantra, a prayer he had learned and was now passing on, as if to an heir.

"The sound of the river has in it every word ever spoken. In it is every life song that has been sung, every cry of pain, every laugh, every sob. Listen to that sound and you'll hear all the answers that you want, they are all in that sound. How can you be lonely with that sound?"

The sun grew more dim and the roar of the river seemed louder. Hayes walked back toward the small stone stove. He picked some small pieces of wood from the pile by the stove and put them on the fire. He knelt down on one knee and leaned into the fire, blowing gently. Light danced on his face and Frank saw the fire grow, flames licking around the fuel that would let it become strong again. Hayes reached over to the pile of wood and put three larger pieces onto the fire. They quickly caught fire and the flame reached high above the grill that lay across the stove. Light filled the camp area. The canopy of branches were all lit and glowing. It seemed to Frank like a room or a building. The branches arched up and Frank couldn't help but think of the church that he went to when he was young. It too had a high roof with large beams of wood reaching up to the sky like fingers. He remembered how at Midnight Mass on Christmas Eve, the church would be lit only by candles. The altar would be filled with pine boughs. The small flickering flames would light the church and the boughs and make the beams seem like huge branches.

Hayes walked over to the small cabin. Through the window in the door Frank could see the old man light a candle with a match. Hayes turned around, looking for something. Having gathered together the things he needed, Hayes walked out of the cabin toward Frank. He had more bread and a small piece of dark brown hard meat. He sat down in front of the stove. Frank sat down as well. Hayes gave Frank a piece of bread. Next, he took out the knife from his pocket and cut the dark meat into six strips. He gave Frank three of these.

"It's moose meat," said Hayes, holding up a piece. "Smoked." Hayes took a bite. It looked to Frank as though he were trying to bite a piece of leather. The old man tugged away at the meat until he managed to rip off a piece. He chewed for a moment then took a piece of the bread. He motioned to Frank. Frank held a piece up to his mouth. It seemed like a piece of softened wood. The outside of the meat felt like bark. Frank tried to bite it. It seemed impossible. Hayes laughed. Frank mimicked Hayes' motions and finally tore off a piece. He chewed it and smiled at Hayes. Hayes laughed again, turning and looking into the fire. His blue eyes flickered with the orange of the flames. Frank wished he had known him as a young man.

"Do you ever think of going back?" he asked, trying to be casual. He noticed that for the first time Hayes' eyes, although still bright, became sad.

"No," said Hayes, his blue eyes flickering. He turned to the fire and bit another piece of moose meat.

"Why not?" asked Frank, pursuing the point.

"I went back once. That was enough," said Hayes. The

logic was pure for him. He said it as if there was no need for further explanation.

"What happened, when you went back?"

Hayes thought for a moment. "Nothing."

"Then why leave again? What drove you away?"

"Nothing," said Hayes again. Frank felt frustrated. It was as though he were speaking to a child.

"Then, why leave? Why leave if nothing happened to force you to go? You had all that was necessary to make a change," said Frank, leaping into the thoughts that he had been keeping deep inside him, too afraid to even think before. "You were a writer and a journalist. You could have made a change for the better. You could have taken the exposure that you had every day and tried to make a change. But you left it," Frank felt his voice grow louder but he could not stop himself. Hayes sat unmoved by his passionate inquiry. "Why? Why leave if you had that ability and that access?" Frank thought about all those student causes that he used to rally around. If only they could get the power to make change, the world would be a better place. He continued. "Why didn't you stay and make them understand. That night with the Jewish boy standing beside you. You could have taken that as a victory but rather you took it as a defeat. Why?" Frank stopped. Had he said too much? He knew better than to let emotion get in the way of a logical argument. Something was in him now, something he couldn't hold back. Hayes was a man who could have made great change.

Hayes' eyes shone blue and Frank felt ashamed of what he had just said. Frank looked into the fire. "I'm sorry about that, I don't know what came over me," he said, trying not to look at Hayes.

"Don't apologize for what you feel," said Hayes. "I think I'm going to turn in. I'll bring out my old tent for you and you can sleep out here. Is that okay?"

Frank looked up at Hayes and nodded. Hayes went back into the cabin and came out with a large pack. He opened it and dumped the contents onto the ground. It was an old canvas tent with aluminum poles. Hayes put the tent up quickly. He went back to the cabin and brought out a blanket for Frank.

"This should keep you warm," said Hayes. "Good night." The old man turned to go back to his cabin. He took a few steps and stopped with his back to Frank.

"You know I was once filled with the questions that you have. I was younger than you, but I did have them. Why is hard. Why leave is even harder. Can anyone explain their world to another? Is that possible? But I stopped asking questions some time ago. It was pointless. Questions lead only to more questions. Instead of questions that begged for more questions and more questions that seemed to never lead to answers, I began to search for the truth. Truth is harder to seek. But the reward of truth is knowing that there is nothing to leave when the world is within you."

Frank couldn't help himself. "Why not go back?"

Hayes' head dropped and he shook it slowly. He turned to face Frank. "I see no need for that."

"Don't you want to know how things have become?"

"I know how things are," said Hayes.

"How?" asked Frank.

"They are as they always have been."

"How do you know?"

Hayes smiled again. With that he turned again and returned to the cabin. After a few seconds, the light in the cabin went out. Frank looked at the fire. There was a dark red glow among the ashes and burnt wood. He put his head in his hands and wiped his forehead. He walked back to the river's edge, and sat down on the bench. The rushing water, barley visible in the darkness, seemed quieter now. Beginning and ending at the same time. He heard Hayes' words over and over again in his head. Frank closed his eyes and listened to the sound of the river. The rush of water continued without pause. The sound seemed smooth and hard at the same time. There was rhythm, and yet, not one.

The words of an old song came to his head: "just being, just being." When Frank opened his eyes, the night seemed bright as day as he looked out on the river. Beginning and ending, beginning and ending. It ran through his head over and over again. Beginning and ending. He thought of the water entering the source of the river, the water that was exiting its mouth. It flowed like time. It was constant. He thought of the cool pools where fish rested and the hard white water that pushed and banged against the side of unfeeling rocks. Beginning and ending, just being. Suddenly, the sounds of the water seemed to become amplified to the point where Frank felt compelled to put his hands over his ears. There was sound everywhere around him. It was not all one sound but layers of sound, not on top of each other but woven together. He heard Willie's voice. Beginning and ending. Just being.

The river woke Frank. He lay in the old green tent and listened to the water. The rushing water on the rocks was like some mother telling the forest to be quiet. Frank lay on his back and wondered how many days the old man must have sat by it, watching it flow. He had spent most of the night sitting by the river, his awe and wonder growing with every minute. One long stream of water that never ended. How he wanted to wake the old man, to tell him that he had doubts. To tell him he heard the river. Now he wondered what he would say to the old man.

Frank wanted him to come back to the city with him. He wanted to take him up to Carlisle's office, and have Hayes standing there as he quit. Stone should be there as well. The two of them would sit with their jaws to the ground, looking at this long-lost man who was their better. A man who could have accomplished more than the two of them put together but who chose rather to discover something else, something real. A smile came to Frank's face as he thought about it. He would take Hayes to Sloan's house. Sloan would be there in his old torn up shorts and shirt. He wondered if the painter would cry.

They would all sit on the patio of Sloan's house and drink gin.

Frank was excited. He wanted to speak to Hayes again. He pulled the covers off and moved to the door. The blanket had been warm and the morning air, even in the tent, was cool. He crawled on his knees to the tent door and pulled the zipper open. As the zipper came down and the tent door flap fell, a world of colour and light opened up. He realized how his senses had been deprived. The brightness of the sun lit the river, and the green and brown water splashed and danced into clouds of white as it ran past the clearing of the woods. The trees, with their bark of white and grey and brown, stood tall, their bright green leaves and needles hanging like jewelry from some model. Frank pulled himself out of the tent and stood up. He stretched and felt the effects of a long and peaceful night's sleep. He rubbed his eyes and looked around the clearing. The old man wasn't at the fire or at his bench by the river. The cabin door was closed. He must still be asleep, thought Frank. He decided to go to the river and wash up. He might even take a swim. The coals and ash had all gone out from the night before. The fire was cold and the wood all gone.

"He'll have to start from scratch again," said Frank to himself.

At the river bank, Frank took off his shirt and put it on the bench. He kneeled and reached his hands into the cold water. He cupped his hands and brought his face down to meet his hands coming out of the river. The water hit his face and it made his body shiver. He rubbed the water on his face. He put his hands into the river again and brought water up to his face. Frank looked at the rushing river. Then, almost without being able to stop himself, he took off his clothes, and in one motion, jumped in. As he hit the water, his whole body shook. At first he felt as though someone had kicked him in the chest. He rolled into a ball and the current took him down the river. He popped his head up and began to swim as hard as he could back toward the bench. Even with that, the bench and the clearing moved from his sight. Frank calmly changed his direction and swam for the shore. Once there, he pulled himself up and out of the water. He stood looking down at the water. Then he looked at his naked body. He folded his arms over his chest and shivered. Then he walked back along the shore to the bench.

Frank dried himself with his shirt and then put his clothes back on. He sat for a moment on the bench. He was smiling. The river went by him, unknowing and uncaring. Beginning and ending. Frank looked across to the other bank. There was a tree with an orange marker tied to it. He hadn't noticed it the day before and wondered why Hayes needed it. He hadn't used any markers to get from the pond to his camp, not orange ones anyway.

Frank sat and stared at the orange marker for a moment. Orange marker. On the tree. Orange marker. His mind was working. His eyes narrowed as he looked at it again. He couldn't take his attention away from it.

He shot out of his seat and Frank ran into the trees, straight for the cabin. He stopped and banged on the door.

"Hayes, Mr. Hayes!" shouted Frank, hoping. Nothing. Frank flung the door opened. He stepped inside. The cabin was empty. Hayes was gone, as was his pack and all his belongings. Frank turned and ran out of the cabin. He went to the stove and without caution, grabbed the ashes from the fire. They were wet and cold. Hayes had put them out. Frank ran to his pack. He threw it on his back and ran to the river, throwing himself into the water. He leapt almost to the middle, his feet reaching out before they touched the bottom. Frank reached the other side and went to the tree with the orange tag. He looked into the forest and saw another tree with an orange tag. Then another past that. He ran into the forest and up the steep slope following the trail that Hayes had left for him.

He rushed into the forest and followed the line of orange tags. He ran as fast as he could and had to stop on a few occasions to catch his breath. Each time, he shook his head in amazement. Why didn't he know? Finally, exhausted, barely able to run, Frank saw a clearing and water. He reached the last tree and walked out onto the rocky shore of the small pond. There was his tent and the remains of his camp fire. Frank walked over to the tent and stood in front of it. He scanned the shore of the pond, stopping at every small shadow and moving tree. He was looking for Hayes, he was hoping to hear a splash. Nothing.

He took his pack off his back and put it on the rock beside his tent. He looked at the tent and realized the zipper had been closed. He had left it open the day before in his rush to follow Hayes into the woods. He knelt down and unzipped the tent. On his sleeping bag was a small piece of paper. He sat down beside his pack.

My young friend,
I hope you aren't angry with me but I've decided that
our meeting should end. My place is here now and it
will always be. Perhaps it always has been. Don't worry
about me rushing away, there is always a home for
someone seeking refuge.

You asked why I don't go back. I wish I could answer
your questions to your satisfaction. Perhaps I will go
back. It is too soon to know, but I am confident.

I dwell, musing at ease beneath the shade
Of spreading bough – o, but tis well with me.

Cecil Rutherford Hayes

p.s. I've taken your bottle of rum. I thought you
wouldn't mind. Thank you.

Frank reached into his bag and smiled, knowing that he was able to give the old man something. He twisted himself around, stretched his legs out on the rock and leaned back on his pack. The sun was on him and he felt warm. He had two days' journey back to the world, a world that would never be the same for him again. He would stay for a while and enjoy the little pond. In the distance he heard the sound of water flowing. Beside it sat a man by a river in the forest.